THE BEDDINGTON INCIDENT

Top Secret Cargo

by BILL FLYNN

ISBN: 1494285746
ISBN-13: 9781494285746

For
My sister, Maryjane (MJ)
&
My daughter, Maryjane (Janey)

ACKNOWLEDGMENTS

My thanks go to remote operated vehicle {ROV) pilot Kevin La Chance, who shared his expertise on deep salvage operations with me. Kevin has been actively involved as an ROV pilot with an ongoing salvage project off Cape Cod.

My thanks, also, go to artist Andy Marino, who provided an illustration for this book.

The following nonfiction book provided me with insight about the successful Alsos Mission during World War Two, headed by Colonel Pash. Pash's mission was staffed with scientists, as well as military members. The mission was responsible for capturing tons of German and Axis uranium as they followed the invading Allies from Italy to Germany. The mission personnel interrogated scientists who were performing atomic energy research. This research was thought to be connected with Hitler's effort to build an atomic bomb.

THE ALSOS MISSION by Boris T. Pash
Published by Award House, 1969

AUTHOR'S NOTE

This book is a work of historical fiction. For the most part, the characters and the events are fictional, but, in some case, events and characterizations follow actual historical occurrences.

CHAPTER I

Gulf of Maine, Atlantic Ocean
July 12, 2013

Flocks of screeching sea gulls follow behind the boat as the net opens to empty a flopping load of cod, haddock, and hake into the trawler's hold. From the wheelhouse, the captain spots a dark object mixed in with the fish that vividly contrasts their light color.

"What in the hell is that black thing that came up in the net with the fish, Antonio?"

"Don't know, Pete. I'll go down and fetch it. Janey, wait till I can climb down and grab it before you ice the catch."

The crew of the *Elizabeth Ann lll* winched up their last haul of fish before returning to their home port of Provincetown on Cape Cod, Massachusetts. Peter Broderick, a fourth generation captain, named after the first captain, his great-grandfather, is at the helm of his 120 foot trawler. The thirty-eight-year-old skipper wears a cap with a long, black visor that captures unruly, blond hair. He throttles down the engine of the trawler to idle with the calloused palm of his right hand.

Pete's swarthy, well-tanned first mate, Antonio Posada, is of Portuguese decent and named after his great-grandfather. His great-grandfather was a crew member on the first *Elizabeth Ann*, which was a first generation Broderick trawler that fished the waters off Cape Cod during the Second World War between 1941 and 1945.

The third member of the crew, Janey Sheffield, who had cast off the name Maryjane in lieu of Janey at an early age, stands by to shovel shaved ice over the fish in the hold. Janey is twenty-two and a graduate of Northeastern University with a degree in marine biology. She works as a deckhand and ship's cook and is eager to gather oceanic, environmental, and fish habitat knowledge during her summer fishing trips. She's looking forward to following in her father's footsteps as a marine biologist.

"Okay, Antonio. Bring that thing forward when you get it, and we'll have a look." Captain Pete makes a note on his logbook. It's the position of the *Elizabeth Ann lll* and the ocean depth where the object came up in the net.

Antonio climbs down a steel ladder attached to the side of the hold. He notices that the black item is speckled with white barnacles. To him, it looks like some kind of package. It's within his reach from the bottom rung on the ladder, so he grasps it and climbs back up to the deck with the object tucked under his left arm. He wipes it down with a towel and places it on the chart table in front of Peter Broderick.

Pete carefully removes most of the barnacles on one side. "Looks like whatever's inside this thing is wrapped in more than one layer of oilskin." He takes out a measuring tape from the chart table drawer. "It's ten inches square and six inches thick. It weighs about seven pounds, and the top layer of oilskin has a thick coat of tar covering it."

"How did it get into our net, Pete?" Janey asks.

"Our net was down about two hundred feet, and the bottom was at four hundred." Pete hefts the package up in both hands. "It must've had some amount of buoyancy. The tidal current at two hundred is running strong. It may've moved back and forth in the current of an incoming and outgoing tide. So that's probably why it came into the net." Pete turns the strange black object over and removes another cluster of barnacles. Antonio and Janey lean over the chart table to get a closer look at some faint red lettering on the black surface.

Pete picks the package up and reads what's written there in faded red letters. "It says *SS BEDDINGTON*, and below, in larger letters, is written TOP SECRET." He points to a flap that's covered by tar. "I think this is where the package was sealed when the tar was hot."

Janey takes a closer look. She is always curious about any strange item coming from the ocean depth. She puts one hand on the tar-covered oilskin and flips her blonde ponytail over one shoulder with the other hand. After she runs her fingers down the sealed seam, she looks up at the captain with an inquisitive expression on her face. Her blue eyes open wide. "Can we open it? I'd love to know what's inside."

"Yeah, I'll get a soldering iron and heat that seam of tar sealing the flap. That'll get it open," Antonio adds.

"Whoa, guys! We will not be opening this package today," Pete says.

Janey's expression changes to frowning disappointment when she says, "Why not?"

"For two reasons…it's marked top secret, and, until it's declassified, it's government property not to be tampered with. The second reason for not opening it now…" Peter Broderick points at the ocean surface. "As a seagoing man, I can't be quick to open something that may've come from a shipwreck with men down there in their graves."

Antonio stares out at the ocean in thought. He recalls a tale about the torpedoing and sinking of the *SS Beddington* passed down through his family from his great-grandfather, the mate on the first *Elizabeth Ann*. "Pete, I remember my father telling me about that ship."

"It, also, rings a bell with me. My great-aunt Annie, the daughter of the first skipper of the *Elizabeth Ann*, told me that her dad rescued some survivors from the *Beddington*. She said, shortly after that, he got a visit from a *navy* officer, telling him to keep quiet about the incident. Annie Broderick is living in Chatham. I'll pay her a visit and try to find out what she recalls about the *Beddington*. After the Coast Guard investigates the top secret classification and declassifies it, I may want to contact the survivors or their relatives."

"That will take some doing. The ship was sunk almost seventy years ago."

"I know, Antonio, but I still want to give it a shot."

Antonio and Janey return to the deck and start to shovel ice into the hold. Pete moves the throttle forward and picks up his ship-to-shore radio microphone as he steers, heading for Provincetown harbor.

Pete tries to call the Coast Guard as the boat reaches a 0.5 nautical miles from where they netted the package. He wants to give them a heads up about the top secret item he'll be delivering when the boat docks. He presses the transmission button on the mike and hears only loud static. He notices that his radar and fish finder scopes are filled with white noise. The other instruments on his console are erratic, as well. Pete quickly throttles back the engine to idle and calls out, "Antonio, come forward and take a look at this stuff!"

Antonio hurries to the bridge. He looks at the scopes and the other instruments. "Holy shit! What's our position?"

Pete reads off the longitude and latitude to Antonio.

"Hey, Pete! I've seen this happen before when we fished around here, but it went away when we moved through it."

Janey joins Pete and Antonio. "What's going on?"

Antonio points at the instruments and the scopes.

"What do you think is causing that, Pete?" she asks.

"It may be some large metal object. Could be the *SS Beddington* down there."

"Or maybe it's something radiating from her cargo hold," Janey says as she takes a small notebook from a breast pocket in her jean jacket and writes down the trawler's position in longitude and latitude and the ocean depth beneath the *Elizabeth Ann lll.*

Pete pushes the throttle forward, and the trawler gets underway. After cruising one hundred yards all scopes and instruments return to normal. Also, the ship-to-shore radio static clears. He contacts the Coast Guard and requests that the duty officer meet the boat at Cabral's Pier in Provincetown.

CHAPTER 2

Provincetown Harbor, the Evening of July 12, 2013

The sun is low on the western horizon as the *Elizabeth Ann lll* approaches Provincetown Harbor at the tip of Cape Cod. It's always a welcome sight for the crew of the *Elizabeth Ann lll* after a long fishing trip to see the stone Pilgrim Monument rising tall above the harbor.

Pete Broderick eases back on the throttle as the boat slips beside the dock at Fisherman's Wharf, also known as Cabral's Pier. Janey jumps onto the dock where Antonio tosses her two ropes to tie the trawler up, bow and stern. After the boat is secured, Pete steps off, carrying the black package with the red letters. A coast guard and a navy officer are waiting for him on the dock.

One of the men is Lieutenant Nathan Howe, an acquaintance of Pete's, from the local Coast Guard station. The other officer, Pete doesn't know.

"Hi, Pete! I'd like you to meet Commander Burrows from the First Naval District office in Boston. He's interested in..." Howe gestures toward the package Pete's carrying. Pete switches it to his left hand and extends his right in anticipation of Burrow's handshake. It doesn't come.

Instead, the commander speaks to him in a terse tone. "Captain Broderick, I must confiscate that package. It is now the property of the United States Navy. I'm asking you not to make mention of finding it to anyone. Is that clear?"

"Not real clear, commander. I assumed that it would be declassified from top secret and returned to me as an artifact that has been recovered at sea. According to this lettering and the information passed on through a relative of mine, this package is from..." Peter says as he points to the faded red lettering on the package, "the *SS Beddington*, a ship sunk by a German U-boat during World War Two."

"Please be advised, Captain Broderick, that the navy and the US government have no record of the sinking of a ship by that name. I must take custody of this package and ask you to treat the matter with the same classification as that marked on the package—top secret. Any breach of security on your part would be considered a serious violation. Please make this known to your crew. I shall take that package now."

Pete thinks about not handing it over for a moment, before he says, "Okay, commander, but I'd like to see your credentials, and I'll need a receipt from you."

Commander Burrows scowls and mumbles something mostly unintelligible that sounds a little like *"Okay, asshole."* He scribbles a receipt on a notebook page, rips it off, and hands it to Pete. Then, he presents his navy identification card. Pete gives him the package, and Burrows leaves the dock followed by Lieutenant Nathan Howe, who catches Pete's inquisitive look. Howe shrugs his shoulders, revealing his lack of understanding about what's going on. The two officers enter a waiting staff car and drive away.

After the catch is off-loaded from the trawler, Pete returns to the boat and asks Antonio and Janey to follow him. He briefs them on what the navy commander told him. "Hey, guys. That package was taken by the navy guy."

"Will you get it back after they declare it no longer classified?'

"At this point, I doubt it, Janey."

"How come?"

"The navy commander made it seem like it would remain government property...not to be returned. In fact, he wanted me to tell you and Antonio not to discuss our finding of it with anyone."

"This is weird, Pete. First, the instruments, scopes, and radio went crazy at the place where we netted the package, and now the navy grabs the thing away from you."

"Yeah, Antonio, but that's not all. According to that navy commander, there is no record of the SS *Beddington* ever being sunk."

"No way, José!"

"I think there's something peculiar going on, like some kind of cover up," Pete adds.

"Why would our government do that?"

"Good question, Janey."

CHAPTER 3

After leaving the dock at Provincetown, Janey Sheffield drives her red Volkswagen Bug the eighty miles to the Sheffield family home in Falmouth. The strange circumstances surrounding the package and the instrumentation disturbance where they netted it play on her mind. Even though, according to Captain Broderick, she is not supposed to mention these incidents, Janey intends to discuss it with her dad.

Ninety minutes after leaving Provincetown, Janey arrives at the gray, cedar-shingled Sheffield home. As she retrieves her backpack from the bonnet, her father, Jay Sheffield, a scientist at the Woods Hole Oceanographic Institute on Cape Cod, walks across the lawn from the patio barbecue where he's grilling steaks. He greets his daughter with a hug.

"How was the fishing trip?"

"Great catch, although some weird stuff happened."

"Okay. Come and take a seat on the patio, grab a cold beer out of the cooler, and tell all."

She tells her father about the mysterious top secret package from the *SS Beddington* and the problem with the scopes, radio, and instruments near where it was netted. She, also, tells that both Pete and Antonio recall tales passed on through their families about the *Beddington* being sunk by a U-boat.

"Where's the package now?"

"That's another bizarre thing, Dad. It was taken away from Pete by a strict navy officer who claimed there wasn't any record of a ship named the *SS Beddington* being sunk by a German sub during World War Two."

Jay Sheffield takes a sip of his beer, flips a steak, and, after a pause in thought, he says, "Tell Peter Broderick to send a letter to the government archives office asking for the package in accordance with the Freedom of Information Act. Also, it wouldn't hurt for him to inform the two Massachusetts senators, who are concerned about our fisheries. That might get some answers for Pete as to why a package marked top secret sixty-eight years ago still remains classified top secret."

Janey takes her iPhone from a pocket in her jean jacket and sends a text message to Captain Peter Broderick, telling him of her dad's suggestions.

While she's texting Pete, Jay opens his laptop on the patio table and Googles it for a list of ships sunk in the Atlantic by U-boats during World War ll. After a few minutes, he says, "A government listing of ships sunk near here does not contain the *SS Beddington*."

"But Peter Broderick said his great-grandfather, the captain of the first *Elizabeth Ann,* knew about that sinking."

"That is strange. How about that interference you saw?"

She reaches in the breast pocket of her jean jacket and hands him the note she'd made on the longitude, latitude, and the depth below the *Elizabeth Ann lll* where that interference was encountered.

"Hmm...I've heard some reports by other boats about that same phenomenon occurring around that position. Might be a good idea for my Woods Hole crew to take a trip out there and drop down a Geiger counter."

"Good...and, on my next fishing trip, I'll get a few fish for you to analyze in the lab near that place where the instruments went wacky. Pete didn't sell the catch that we hauled near that interference. It's been placed in cold storage until we know what's going on."

"That's a good move on Pete's part."

"What do you think was causing the instruments to go crazy?"

"Can't hazard a guess, but we had similar activity on surface instrumentation when I was checking on *the* deep ocean atomic waste dumps in the Pacific with our submersible vehicle, *Alvin*[1]."

"How deep was that operation?"

Jay Sheffield looks at Janey's note on the ocean depth below the *Elizabeth Ann lll* at the time of the disturbance. "We were working with *Alvin* in ocean depths much deeper than where you saw that interference. Our deployments were over two miles at those atomic waste dump locations. We were looking for any leaking radioactive material from containers."

"Are there any of those atomic waste dumps off Cape Cod?"

"To my knowledge, there hasn't been any atomic waste dumping around Cape Cod and none in the Gulf of Maine." He looks again at the note she gave him on the position of the *Elizabeth Ann lll* when the interference was observed. "I suppose you could see a magnetic effect that strong from a metal ship at a depth of four hundred feet, but that would only bother a ship's compass...not those other instruments."

"Could you use *Alvin* to look for the *SS Beddington?*"

"The navy owns it, and, according to that naval officer's attitude when he confiscated the package, my getting their permission to deploy *Alvin* would be problematic."

"Oh! By the way, I wasn't supposed to tell you about any of this stuff."

---

[1] Alvin, the deep submergence vehicle, is named for Allyn Vine, a Woods Hole geophysicist who helped pioneer deep ocean diving research and development.

"What stuff, Janey?"

First, she smiles in reaction to that question. Then, her expression becomes serious. "I'd really like to know more about that package, the *Elizabeth Ann lll's* instrumentation interference, and the sinking of the *SS Beddington*."

Jay Sheffield takes a sip of beer and turns another steak over on the barbecue grill. Then, he says, "So would I."

CHAPTER 4

Washington, DC, November 19, 1943

Major General Leslie Grove, head of the US atomic bomb effort, known as the Manhattan Project, has been called to a meeting at the War Department by Secretary of War Henry L. Stimson.

The secretary opens the meeting and is first to speak. "Leslie, I'm tapping you to organize and command a group of army personnel and atomic scientists for a special mission."

"If you don't mind my saying so, Mr. Secretary, that's a strange combination for me to put together."

"I know, but an important one. Hitler, under the pressure of Allied might, is threatening to unleash his super weapons. According to intelligence, it's suspected that one might be an atomic explosive. I'll let General Casey outline the mission for you."

Casey stands up from the conference table and walks to a podium in front of it. He puts a chart up on an easel with his handwritten words on it. He points to the first sentence and starts to speak.

"The mission is threefold, General Grove. Number one: To scientifically evaluate the progress of German research toward the building of an atomic bomb. Two: To interrogate and capture the European scientists researching what could lead to developing an atomic bomb. We may want to send those scientists to the United States to be employed on the Manhattan Project. Three: To find uranium ore that is staged for atomic bomb development in German-occupied Europe and ship it to the United States."

General Casey leaves the podium and takes his seat at the conference table where he continues to address General Grove.

"That third part of the mission is critical. The uranium that's assumed to be stored in eastern Germany could come into the hands of the Russian Armed Forces as they make their drive toward Berlin. Do you have any questions, General Grove?"

"No, but I would like to add to your point about the critical aspect of the mission. In addition to keeping the uranium away from the Russians, we have an urgent need at Oak Ridge for any uranium ore that's captured. My Manhattan Project is running short on uranium ore, and we need all we can get."

Grove's comment prompted annoyance from Secretary of War Stimson. "What the hell is going on, Grove? My reports have shown that we have enough of that stuff, and we've spent millions to get it."

"Mr. Secretary, if I may? Uranium ore, as mined, makes up less than one percent of that needed to process it into weapons-grade or isotope U-235, which is needed to build an atomic bomb."

"You're telling me, Grove, that we need German uranium ore to build an atomic bomb to drop on the Japs? By the way, gentlemen, what I just said is not to leave this room. How're you going to get that uranium to Oak Ridge?"

"I'll order the mission to make high priority shipments to the United States of all uranium ore or weapons-grade material captured in Germany and German-Occupied Europe, Mr. Secretary."

"Do you have anyone in mind to carry out this mission of yours in Europe?" Stimson asks.

"Yes, sir. I do. I'll give the in-country mission assignment to Lieutenant Colonel Boris Pash."

"Tell me about this Boris Pash and why you chose him."

"He holds a master's degree in engineering and speaks several languages. Pash worked with the scientists on the Manhattan Project at Los Alamos, Oak Ridge, and Berkley. As you know, sir, handling a dozen civilian scientists, not tuned in to the military way, will be a daunting task, and I think Pash is up to that job."

"Good, General Grove. I would like you to start the mission in Italy where the Allies have just landed. I will make sure that your mission gets top priority from all of our European commanders." The war secretary smiles. "Casey has coined a name for your mission. We shall call it *Alsos*. He says it's the Greek word for *grove*."

CHAPTER 5

Boris Pash, with his detachment of troops and scientists in tow, has followed the invading Allies throughout Occupied Europe and into Germany. His detachment has confiscated uranium ore in Italy, France, and Belgium. The Alsos Mission personnel has interrogated European scientists involved in processing atomic material, and, in some cases, they've captured those scientists and sent them to the United States. Strassfurt would be the last stop for the Alsos Mission personnel.

Pash and Doctor Jack Springer, one of his scientists, are pinned down by German sniper fire on the outskirts of Strassfurt.

"Boris, is getting shot a part of my contract?" Doctor Springer asks while they're crouched down behind a building as another bullet ricochets nearby.

"Not at the present moment, Jack, but I can add it."

"Will you issue me a weapon?"

"But you're a conscientious objector, Jack."

"I, also, conscientiously object to being shot at, Boris."

* * *

After the 83rd Infantry Division secured Strassfurt, the Alsos Mission occupied a two-story farmhouse. The ten-room fieldstone structure is a comfortable reprieve for the men after living in the field for the past two months. A fireplace roars and spreads its warmth toward a large oak table where the scientists and military staff sit.

It was time for a promotion party, followed by a meeting. One of the men had confiscated three bottles of cognac when they'd passed through France. The cognac is poured into some earthen mugs found in the kitchen and a toast to Colonel Pash is in order.

Lieutenant Colonel Pash has been promoted to full colonel. The scientists were given the honorary rank of colonel at the start of the Alsos Mission to recompense them for being "drafted" to serve the country with their atomic energy knowledge.

Although short in stature and wearing round, wire-rimmed, army- issued glasses, Pash shows a military bearing. He stands straight beside the table and speaks to his men. "I am now of equal rank to you scientists."

This brings a laugh from the men sitting around the harvest table in the farmhouse den. They'd always responded to Pash's direction when he was a lieutenant colonel, regardless of their elevated status of colonel.

Pash continues to address the group. "Gentlemen, our intelligence sources have reported that the mother lode of uranium ore has been stored here in the Strassfurt caves by the Nazis. The Alsos Mission has been successful all the way from Italy to here. This will be the last phase of our mission, so we shall make it the best. Now, let's get all that uranium ore out of here before the Russians arrive. Thank you."

* * *

Two days later, after the Alsos Mission had located all the uranium ore stored in Strassfurt and readied it for shipment, Pash called another meeting.

"Gentlemen, the amount of uranium ore hidden by the Nazis in the caves of Strassfurt turned out to be much more than we anticipated. There's even some metalized uranium ingots that have been processed by a German 'uranium machine.' The uranium ore is stored in wooden barrels made of oak staves with steel bands around them. The metalized uranium ingots are in those same barrels."

Jack Springer says, "What's your estimate of the total, Boris?"

"Over one thousand tons."

Sounds of surprise come from the men sitting around the table when they hear that tonnage number.

"Christ! How the hell do we get that amount out of here and shipped to the states, Boris?"

"Jack and all, my first plan was for the Royal Air Force to airlift the ore from a recently captured airfield in Hanover to Avonmouth, England. But one thousand tons is too much weight for that plan."

"So, where do we go from here?" another scientist sitting at the table asks.

Colonel Pash looks down at some notes in front of him. "We'll split the shipment. The one hundred tons of uranium ore and the one ton of metalized uranium will be trucked to Hanover and flown to Avonmouth by the Brits. Once there, a ship will be standing by to take it to the Port of Boston, Massachusetts, where it will be flown to Oak Ridge."

Posh is interrupted by an army lieutenant. "Sir, my men got something that looks like slight burns on their hands when handling those wooden barrels with the metalized uranium ingots inside. Is that stuff hot?"

"We don't know much about the effect of radiation on skin yet, Brown, but we'll treat those as normal skin burns for now. Also, we'll place red caution tags on those barrels where the metalized uranium ingots are stored."

Posh looks back down at his notes. "The other nine hundred tons of ore will be shipped to Antwerp, Belgium, by truck and sent by ship from there to the Port of Charleston, South Carolina. From there, it'll be trucked to Oak Ridge. An army company of truckers known as the *Red Ball Express* will do all the transporting by land here in Europe. Are there any questions, gentlemen?"

Jack Springer asks the question on the mind of all those around the table. "When can we, the Alsos Mission people, go home, Boris? I'd like to paint my last KILROY WAS HERE[2] symbol in this house like the ones I did on all the other places in Europe where Alsos has been lodged."

Posh answers him. "Get your paintbrush ready, Jack. Alsos will leave for the states very soon. My thanks to all of you for a job well-done."

With that announcement, a happy roar came from all the men, followed by loud applause.

---

[2] *KILROY WAS HERE is an American expression, started by a ship inspector, by the name of Kilroy, in Fore River, Massachusetts, as he marked poorly made rivets with this character. It caught on with sailors and soldiers. Its graffiti, popular during World War Two, became associated with the GIs as they made their way through Europe. Kilroy was sketched or painted on the walls of many buildings as the invading American soldiers passed. This simple drawing of a bald-headed man with a prominent nose peeking over a wall was seen almost everywhere GIs were lodged, as well as in train stations and other European public buildings.*

CHAPTER 6

Avonmouth, England... April 17, 1945

The *SS Beddington* had just finished taking on a secret Lend-Lease payback cargo of precious metals dropped off by a Russian vessel when it was placed on standby to receive another classified cargo. The British owned, 420 foot, refrigerated cargo ship would depart Avonmouth for Halifax, Nova Scotia, on April 18. From there, it would be escorted to Boston as part of convoy XB 32.

* * *

Two dock workers, Alfie and Nigel, are savoring their second pint at Avonmouth's Red Rooster Pub after a hard two days of loading cargo onboard the *SS Beddington*. Their sleeveless, muscled, and tattooed arms are gesturing in a three-way conversation with the bartender. They talk loud to make their points, and they ignore those words of warning posted above the bar—*"A slip of the lip could sink a ship."*

"Alfie and I near broke our bloody backs handling that cargo off the Russian ship and onto that *SS Beddington*," Nigel tells the bartender.

"Righto, mate, and then comes along another secret, hushed-up bunch of wooden barrels that are even heavier that the Russian stuff," Alfie adds.

"Yeah, what's it all about, Alfie? How about that dispatcher bloke telling us that both the cargo from the Russian ship and those barrels that came later were miscellaneous auto parts? Auto parts, my arse! Each of those barrels weighed more than thirty stone, and those others from Russia were just as heavy. Do you think all those military chaps were there just to guard against us getting a peak at some auto parts?"

"That's not the all of it, Nigel. How about a few of our mates getting their hands burnt when handling some of those bloody barrels that came to the dock from the airfield?"

"Righto. And that dispatcher bloke told us to ignore those red warning tags on those five barrels."

Five stools down, Richard Smyth is listening to the conversation between Alfie, Nigel, and the bartender. Smyth is a frequent patron of the Red Rooster and a casual acquaintance of Alfie and Nigel. He joins in on their conversation.

He buys Alfie and Nigel their third pint and moves down a few stools. After they thank him for the beer, Smyth says, "You chaps have had a hard day loading that heavy cargo, and you deserve a little relaxation." He toasts them with his shot glass of Irish whiskey. "Those barrels you loaded weighed in at over thirty stone each, you say? Bloody tough to move them around, I'd say."

Nigel takes a large gulp from his pint. "It was no fun, Richard."

"After you finished the Russian bunch, how many of those barrels did your chaps load?"

Nigel looks over at Alfie. "I counted five hundred barrels, and five of those barrels had those red tags that the dispatcher told us not to worry about."

Alfie nods in agreement with the number.

Smyth buys Nigel and Alfie another pint. "I'd like to spend more time with you chaps, but there's a splendid little bird I must meet. Tallyho, and have a smashing evening."

"Now, it wouldn't be that shapely, widowed landlady of yours, would it?" Nigel asks. "Many a bloke in this town would like to get next to her."

Richard Smyth leaves the pub for his nearby rooming house. He opens the front door of the gray, three-story building and bounds up the stairs, taking two steps at a time, until he reaches the second floor landing. He inserts a key in the door to his room and enters. Once inside, he performs a quick calculation, converting the British thirty-stone weight for each barrel times the five hundred barrels Nigel mentioned. He comes up with a number to approximate the one hundred tons of uranium that Berlin intelligence had said was shipped from Strassfurt and airlifted via Hanover to an airstrip near Avonmouth.

He smirks while thinking, *The Red Rooster is a very lucrative place to attain information on shipments leaving the Port of Avonmouth for America. Only yesterday, a loose-lipped first mate from the ship that brought a precious metal cargo to Avonmouth from Russia boasted about it during some bar talk at the Red Rooster. That gold and platinum cargo was transferred to the SS Beddington from the Russians' ship.*

Smyth opens a closet door and lifts a floorboard where a shortwave transmitter and receiver are located. He turns on the battery operated radio and taps out a coded message to Berlin: *SS Beddington took on Strassfurt cargo. Sails on eighteenth via Halifax to Boston also with aforementioned precious metals from Russia…Scorpion out.*

Otto Brünner, alias Richard Smyth with the code name of Scorpion, puts his radio back under the floorboard. He places a laundry bag over it and makes note of the position in case it's lifted by his nosey landlord. Otto hears a board creak outside the door to his room. He looks up at a shelf where his Luger pistol is hidden beneath some clothing. He hesitates for a moment, staring at the shelf, before he rushes from the closet to the door and flings it open.

His landlord, Mary Conroy, stands there with her fist raised as if preparing to knock. She's dressed in a tight fitting summer dress that shows all of her body..

"Oh! Hello, Mister Smyth...you startled me. I came to knock you up and ask if you'd like to join me for dinner and drinks at seven. I'm serving Yorkshire pudding."

Otto catches a whiff of her perfume. His eyes travel the length of Mary's enticing figure, and they pause at her cleavage.

"Okay. Thanks. I'll be down in half an hour."

As Otto shaves his face, he thinks about Mary Conroy. *"She's nosey, asks too many questions, and snoops around a lot. I may have to kill her... but not until I have my way with her."*

* * *

After their dinner with wine, Mary stands up from the table to start taking away the dishes. Otto seizes her with his arms. His rough embrace forces her body to press against his, and his lips meet hers with a firm kiss.

She breaks away from his crushing grip and says, "Oh, my! Mister Smyth...I never thought...perhaps, we should go to the divan in the parlor."

In the parlor, Otto throws Mary on the divan and lands on top of her. He presses another rough kiss on her lips, and his hands grope at her breasts.

Mary reaches behind a cushion on the couch for a pistol she'd hidden earlier. She shoots Otto once in the heart. After she stands, she fires a second bullet. It penetrates his crotch. She says, "You

Nazi bastard, this is for my husband that your SS friends shot in the back at Dunkirk." She waves the pistol in his face. "I found your transmitter in the closet, you rotten spy, and this gun of yours hidden on its shelf."

There's a loud knock at the door. Mary walks across the room to answers it. When she opens the door, two policemen are standing on the threshold. One says, "We got a call telling us that a German spy is living here. Where is he?"

"He's lying on my divan in the parlor, dead."

CHAPTER 7

0600, the next morning, April 18, onboard the SS Beddington.

The ship's master, Phillip Ramsey, is on the bridge, making preparations to leave the Port of Avonmouth. It would be the tenth wartime crossing of the Atlantic for the forty-nine-year-old, pipe smoking, and slightly graying captain. So far, his ship had avoided the German U-boat onslaught. His chief officer, Harold Walker, puts a steaming mug of tea on the chart table for his captain and reports on the ship's readiness to leave the dock.

"Sir, the tide will be right to get us underway at 0700. All is ready, and those so-called miscellaneous auto parts, as shown on this manifest, are loaded and secure." He places a copy of the manifest on the chart table.

Phillip Ramsey puffs on his white meerschaum pipe. His eyes squint as they look at his chief officer. "Harold, this is a fake manifest used by our intelligence chaps to hide the real contents of our cargo. They had a force of around fifteen army guards making sure the dock workers and our crew didn't get too curious. Five of those guards are going to make the trip with us."

The ship's master reaches down to a steel safe below the chart table. He twirls the combination three times to unlock it. Ramsey, then, places a package coated with oilskin and sealed with black tar on the chart table. On the package in red letters is written SS BEDDINGTON and, below that, TOP SECRET.

"A chap from MI6 dropped this off yesterday with instructions to hand it over to an American navy captain by the name of Sanders when we dock in Boston. Now, Harold, this package most likely contains the manifest telling what we really have as cargo onboard."

"Righto, sir. I believe it does. Five of the barrels had red caution tags attached. Have no idea what was in them, but that same chap from MI6 insisted that the dock workers put those five barrels in hold number three, our dangerous cargo hold. He, also, ordered the other 495 barrels to be loaded in holds one and two and for the cargo from that Russian ship be put in number four."

"Good place for those five barrels, Harold. They're above the waterline and close to the top deck, in case what's in there explodes. Did you lock up hold three?"

"Yes, sir, and I put an off-limits sign on the hatches to keep the crew and guards away. Also, some dock workers received burns on their hands when they handled those barrels."

* * *

An hour later, the *SS Beddington* leaves the dock. After the ship clears the harbor, it heads for Halifax, Nova Scotia.

With the Port of Avonmouth behind him, the ship's master takes a long drag on his pipe and speaks to his chief officer. "Well, Harold, if we can make twelve knots and not encounter any U-boats, we'll be outside Halifax on the afternoon of the twenty-sixth. It will be on to Boston for arrival the morning of the twenty-eighth."

* * *

Onboard the SS Beddington, outside Halifax Harbor, April 26, 1945
Walker reports, "We have the freighter, *SS Algonquin*, off our port side; a US Navy destroyer and a Canadian corvette are standing by as escorts, sir. We should be ready to get underway soon."

"Not yet, Harold. We're waiting for two more warships as part of convoy XB-32."

"Four warships escorting two freighters? That seems a bit much, sir."

"I know, but that's probably because of our secret cargo."

An hour later another, a Canadian corvette and a United States Coast Guard cutter arrive, and convoy XB-32 leaves Halifax Harbor and heads for the Gulf of Maine on the way to the Port of Boston.

CHAPTER 8

The German U-boat base in Lorient, France
April 26, 1945

Kapitänleutnants Karl Heineke and Günter Godt are in the map room at the German U-boat fleet headquarters, plotting the position of their U-boats in the Atlantic.

"It's almost over, Karl. This place changed from a fully occupied U-boat base to empty pens with only a skeleton crew."

"The silence is eerie. But, if it weren't for General Fahrmbacher and his army of fifteen thousand men, this base would've been overrun by the Americans."

"Maybe. The French and American armies were ignoring us when they rushed toward their victors' rewards in Paris." Günter leaves the map wall and stares out a large picture window at the empty U-boat pens in Lorient Harbor. "Anyway, there's not much left after those bunker buster bombs were dropped. Hard to imagine that we once had twenty U-boat pens out there, and now there's nothing but rubble left."

A flustered staff member bursts into the map room and blurts out, "Sirs, Grand Admiral Dönitz is on the phone from Berlin."

Heineke and Godt go to an office where a speaker is connected to the admiral's phone call. Günter talks into it. "Hello, admiral sir."

"Hello, Günter. Is Karl Heineke with you?"

"I'm here, admiral."

"Good. I'm calling from Herr Hitler's bunker in Berlin, and he's very angry about the Americans taking uranium ore from

Strassfurt. That uranium was to be used to make one of his secret weapons. A report from our man in England says it was loaded on a British ship headed for America. The Führer wants that ship 'blown out of the water,' and those are his very words."

"Do you have the name of the ship, sir?" Heineke asks.

"Yes, it's the SS *Beddington,* and it left Avonmouth, England, on the eighteenth."

"We know about that ship, sir," Heineke says. "We got a report two days ago from the Gestapo in Berlin that it's carrying precious metals from Russia and headed for America by way of Halifax. We've considered it a prime target for *U-873,* which is on patrol near its suspected route."

"Very well, men. Consider that ship a target of the highest priority. That's an order. Also, I must tell you that Germany will surrender soon. I worked with you both at Lorient and want you to be safe. Destroy all records, leave Lorient, and join with General Fahrmbacher, who will surrender his garrison soon. Also, our Atlantic U-boat fleet has only bombed out pens to return to at Lorient and our other bases. When our capitulation is final, I want you to order our boats to surrender to the Americans at sea."

Both kapitänleutnants say, "Yes, sir" and, with that, the admiral's call ends.

"Our Führer is very upset about the loss of his uranium ore. How about that surrender at sea that the admiral mentioned?"

"We've lost this war, Günter. This could be the admiral's last order to us, so let's contact *U-873* with a coded [3]enigma message to

---

[3] ENIGMA is the name given to a code developed by the Germans to communicate with their military. The enigma encrypted devices or machines were located in U-boats and were key to their receiving and transmitting operational messages. Unknown to the Germans the code was broken by a British team with assistance from Polish mathematicians. The Germans could not conceive that their enigma code was compromised and continued sending messages. Some say that factor won the war for the Allies.

execute it. Hopefully, the Allies have not broken our enigma code that we use to contact all our U-boats. It's a sad ending for Admiral Dönitz. He lost two of his sons and thousands of his U-boat crews without gaining an ultimate victory in this damn war."

"Yeah, the past successes of his U-boat fleet were all for naught. Do you know the captain of *U-873*, Karl?"

"We served the fleet in 1942 during the happy days of Operation Drumbeat. Heinz Haupt is the best."

CHAPTER 9

U-873 is cruising on the surface, eighty-five nautical miles off the coast of Maine, while its batteries are being charged.

The captain, Oberleutnant Heinz Haupt, is on deck with his second-in- command, Gerhardt Meyer. Haupt wears a long, leather coat. The cap that's crushed down on his head is white without starch. A black beard that's been growing for two months covers his face. Both men are scanning the horizon with their binoculars. The sea is calm and visibility is good.

Gerhardt Meyer is not as tall as his captain. He wears a black wool watch cap on his head that's pulled down over his eyebrows. His leather jacket collar covers his chin. Gerhardt tosses a half-smoked cigarette overboard. "According to the boatswain, we're in position to intercept and engage our target ship heading for Boston from Halifax, captain. It should arrive near here in two or three hours, according to the information we have on when the convoy left Halifax."

"Good. My communication from Lorient tells me the *SS Beddington* will be escorted by convoy. Our sonar operator will most likely hear the screws loud and clear from all those ships before we make visual sightings. If it's a large convoy, we'll follow behind it until we can get in position to fire our torpedoes with a broadside shot at the target ship. After, if the escort ships haven't found us and start dropping their depth charges, we'll seek other targets."

"Can we identify that primary target ship, sir?"

"The information I got from Heineke in Lorient is that the *SS Beddington* is a refrigerator cargo ship at over eight thousand tons, 480 feet long with a beam of sixty-two feet. Its cargo is uranium ore and precious metals from Russia, speculated to be tons of gold and platinum. In an enigma follow-up message, Heineke gave me some information on the ship's silhouette he took from a Lloyd's of London photograph."

"What does Kapitänleutnant Heineke say about the war?"

"Germany will soon capitulate according to what Admiral Dönitz told him. Heineke says the U-boat fleet now in the Atlantic will surrender to the American navy and be escorted to an American port." Heinz Haupt removes his binoculars, and, with a piercing look, he holds Meyer's eyes with his own. More to bolster his own resolve, he says, "Gerhardt, we are still at war, and we must conduct ourselves accordingly." He looks at his watch. "It's time to submerge and wait for our quarry to arrive."

They clear the deck, scramble through the hatch, and down the ladder. Meyer always dreads the change from the fresh ocean air on deck to the stench below—diesel fumes, rotten vegetables, and the smell cast off by forty-three men who have not bathed properly in over two months.

Both men duck their way through a labyrinth of overhead, scalp-seeking pipes and valves before they take their command position in the control room. The crew members nearby always watch their captain's expression at the start of an engagement. Haupt's look is calm and encouraging without fear, and that mannerism is instilled in the men around him. Haupt's orders start to sound out.

"Flood ballast tanks!"

"Stern up seven degrees!"

"Bow down seven degrees!"

"Level off at periscope depth!"

"Up periscope!"

Haupt scans the horizon for ten minutes. He repeats that survey of 360 degrees every five minutes for an hour. There's no convoy in sight. He touches a switch to lower the periscope and asks his radioman, "Fritz, any contact?"

Fritz is concentrating on a weak pinging sound coming through his earphones. He turns a wheel slightly to move the antenna until he finds a stronger signal. The pinging sound peaks at 295 degrees, and he tells the captain that. Haupt orders the helmsman to change course.

"Course correction to 292 degrees."

"Up periscope!"

Haupt searches a narrow section around the U-boat's new heading. An outline of six ships in convoy appears, highlighted by the setting sun from the west. The periscope comes down, and he orders, "Go to battle stations!"

Haupt, with pen in hand, sketches out his change in tactic on a sheet of paper at the chart table while talking to Meyer. "Our two targets are escorted by four warships." He draws a crude representation of the warships and the two freighters and points to the smallest one. "This freighter is smaller than the *Beddington*. I want to launch a torpedo against that vessel to cause confusion and diversion." He presses his pen down hard against his sketch of the larger freighter and says, "Then, we'll go after the *Beddington.*"

The periscope goes back up, and Haupt orders, "Change course to 252 degrees!" That position places the bow of *U-873* broadside to the convoy as it passes by. Haupt watches as a gap between the escort ships to the target appears in the periscope optics.

Haupt's next command is: "Flood torpedo tubes one and four!"

Haupt sights the periscope on the smaller freighter, and the bow of *U-873* is now pointed toward the *SS Algonquin* at midship.

The command the crew's been waiting for comes from their captain.

"Fire one!"

The torpedo is launched, and a trail of white phosphorous foam tracks toward the *Algonquin* until an explosion and fireball confirms a direct hit. While the escort ships are busy rescuing survivors and searching for his U-boat, Haupt quickly orders *U-873* into a position to launch two torpedoes at his next target—the *SS Beddington.*

CHAPTER 10

The ship's master, Ramsey, and his chief officer, Walker, are standing on the bridge of the *Beddington*, watching a burning oil slick where the *Algonquin* went down.

"The *Algonquin* is gone, sir. She must have taken a hit right at her fuel tanks."

"We're not in a position to pick up survivors, Harold. Looks like our escorts have that well in hand, and they've moved away from us. There's a U-boat out there, and its torpedoes are aimed at us. Tell the crew to close all compartments and get the men below up on deck. Prepare to abandon ship."

Walker is on the intercom and has just completed Ramsey's order when he spots two white phosphorous trails heading for the ship. He points to them and yells at his captain, "Two torpedoes coming at us from 186 degrees."

The helmsman makes a desperate try to steer the ship's large mass away from the two trails of white foam coming straight at them. Too late...one torpedo hits the center of the *Beddington*. The other makes its impact aft, near the engine room. Both are lethal blows.

As the ship shudders from the torpedo impact and explosion, Ramsey orders, "Abandon ship!"

The crew dashes to the lifeboats, and they're lowered. Some climb down rope ladders and swim frantically toward the nearby vessels. Ramsey and Walker watch that ghastly scene unfold from the bridge. They see a burning oil slick, and their men rowing and swimming toward rescue boats.

"Most of our men are being hauled out of the water by the corvette's crew."

"Good, Harold. Our men missed having to pass through that burning oil slick from the *Algonquin*." They hear a siren blaring from the destroyer as it passes by the wounded SS *Beddington*. "The destroyer *Greenleaf* is racing off to find and sink that U-boat. I hope they get that bastard. Now, let's get the hell out of here."

"But she's still afloat, sir."

"Over the side, now, Harold, and that's an order."

* * *

Ramsey and Walker watch from their lifeboat as the rescue efforts are centered on where the *Algonquin* went down. "I don't think they all made it off before she sunk. Did all our men make it, Harold?"

"I believe all but two men in the engine room. They didn't get up on deck before the torpedoes hit. And look, the *Beddington* hasn't gone down yet."

"She's a tough, old bird, Harold."

* * *

Peter Broderick, captain of the *Elizabeth Ann*, points the bow toward the smoke and flame coming from the *Algonquin* and *Beddington*. He calls for his mate, Antonio Posada, to come to the bridge. "Looks like a U-boat attacked some ships, Antonio." Peter points to the northeast. "Winch in the net, I'm going to get over there and see if we can help."

The trawler bounds through the swells at full speed, toward the smoke and flame. Before it gets close to the chaotic scene of fire, smoke, and men in the water, Peter spots a lifeboat with five men in it, rowing toward them. "Okay, Antonio. Let's get them onboard."

He maneuvers the *Elizabeth Ann* to a position next to the boat, and Antonio hauls each of the men onto the trawler's deck. The last one Antonio helps board has sergeant chevrons on his sleeve.

"I'm Sergeant Richard Collins. We're British army guards off the *SS Beddington*. She took two torpedoes broadside. We all got in a lifeboat and rowed like hell away from there." He introduces the others. All had happy-to-be-rescued smiles on their faces, except Private James Lawson. The boy of eighteen has an expression of bewilderment or shock on his face.

"Antonio, see if we still have that bottle of Irish whiskey we've saved for medicinal purposes."

The army guards, each wrapped in blankets, are seated on deck with their backs against the wheelhouse bulkhead. They sip whiskey from coffee cups while Peter hails the destroyer *Greenleaf* on their frequency.

The destroyer *Greenleaf* responds, and Peter transmits, "*Greenleaf, this is Captain Peter Broderick, Elizabeth Ann out of Provincetown. I've rescued five British Army men off Beddington. Do you want them transferred to you, and do you want to have the Elizabeth Ann standby for other rescue efforts?*"

There's a pause before the answer is radioed back.

"*Elizabeth Ann. . .negative on standby efforts. Please proceed with the survivors to Provincetown.*"

Peter tells the five men, "You are going to Cape Cod."

Sergeant Collins speaks for his men. "Captain Broderick, we will be pleased to be on any dry land. We are soldiers, not sailors."

Peter smiles. "You are five lucky landlubbers to have escaped that ship."

"Yes, if it wasn't for the *Beddington's* ship's master, we wouldn't be here. He ordered all compartments closed and got us up on deck before the torpedoes hit."

* * *

The corvette reaches the lifeboat carrying Ramsey and Walker with four of their crew. They're brought onboard and given a steaming mug of tea and a shot of rum.

All on the corvette watch in the distance as geysers spout near where the navy destroyer is pummeling the Nazi U-boat with depth charges.

CHAPTER II

After the second torpedo hit the *SS Beddington*, a loud cheer rose up from the crew of the *U-873*. The excitement soon eases when the sonar operator raises his hand for silence. Through his earphones, he hears the telltale pings of a destroyer's propellers. He tells Captain Haupt, "Sir, there's a destroyer closing fast toward us. It's at a range of three hundred meters."

Haupt orders a crash dive to 150 meters. All crew that are not at a control station rush forward, so their weight will enhance the dive down angle.

"Rig for depth charges" is the captain's next order.

The first pass by the destroyer is a brutal one. Seawater spouts from valves, pipe joints, and a ballast tank, and two torpedo tubes are reported as damaged by the engineer. The U-boat takes a pounding for five minutes more, and this prompts Haupt to makes a decision.

"Helmsman, take us down to 260 meters."

First Officer Meyer rolls his eyes and looks over at Haupt with an expression of concern. "Captain, this boat's hull is designed only to withstand the pressure at a crush depth of 250 meters."

Haupt reads Meyer's expression and his concern. "It's all right, Gerhardt. Surely, our good German designers of the hull left a crush tolerance safety margin."

When the U-boat reaches 260 meters, the crew hears metallic groaning and clanging sounds throughout the boat caused by outside water pressure against the hull. Their apprehension peaks, although there is no panic.

Haupt asks the engineer for a damage report.

"Except for that reported earlier, sir, we have some valves and pipes leaking from the concussion and pressure, but those are under control."

Haupt looks over at Meyer, who seems to be holding his breath.

"Okay. That last depth charge barrage fell short," Haupt yells out to all in the control room. "Their charges aren't set to detonate at 260 meters. I'll wait out two more passes for the same depth charge shortfall from that destroyer. After that, we'll make the kit ready to launch."

After the waiting period, Haupt says, "Prepare the kit, Gerhardt."

Meyer makes up the kit in a torpedo-shaped canister. He pours in twenty gallons of diesel fuel, along with some typical U-boat odds and ends and some trash and clothing. The canister is launched from torpedo tube number four. All onboard *U-873* hope and pray that when the oil-slick and debris reach the surface, it will appear to the destroyer's crew that they've made a lethal U-boat hit.

After the kit is launched, there are no more depth charge passes by the destroyer, and Haupt says, "I believe the fake debris did its deed, but we'll wait an hour before going to periscope depth and having a look around."

During the hour wait, it's a quiet boat crew with the exception of those sounds coming from the water pressure against the hull. The crew is silent. Some have prayers of thanks for surviving another depth charge attack.

The U-boat rises to periscope depth. Haupt raises the periscope and scans the horizon for 360 degrees. He tells all in the control room. "There's no sign of the destroyer." A sigh of relief from all is heard. One sailor lets out a loud cheer, and another whistles. "The only other warship left is a corvette, but the *SS Beddington* is sitting low in the water and has not gone down. We'll save our three torpedoes for further action. A surface shelling is too risky. With the damage we've made to that ship, I think she will soon sink."

Haupt records the longitude and latitude of the SS Beddington's position and says to Meyer, "Let's get out of here to await our fate. The order to surrender this U-boat will be coming to us from Lorient soon."

CHAPTER 12

The duty officer receives an urgent message from the First Naval District in Boston. He phones his commanding officer, Admiral Ballard, at home.

"Sir, we have a report from First Naval that the *Algonquin* and *Beddington* have been attacked by a U-boat in the Gulf of Maine, eighty-five nautical miles off Portland."

Commander Fouracre had awaken the admiral from a sound sleep. It took a moment for him to get his bearings. After ten seconds, the duty officer hears a raspy voice over the phone ask, "Have they both been sunk?"

"No, sir. The *Algonquin* went down with heavy casualties, but the *Beddington* is still afloat. All except two crew members were rescued from it."

There's a pause before the admiral speaks. "Where's the captain of the *Beddington* now?"

"He's onboard the *Ingalls*. It's the Canadian corvette that rescued him. The *Ingalls* is standing by."

"The *Beddington* is carrying a top secret cargo that is very important to our war effort, Commander Fouracre. Send a message to the corvette ordering the *Beddington* captain to go back onboard to evaluate the salvage possibilities. Get back to me when that's confirmed."

CHAPTER 13

Onboard the corvette, Ingalls, 0455 hours, April 28, 1945

Ramsey, the *Beddington's* ship's master, is lying on a bunk in the corvette captain's quarters trying to sleep, but the tragic events of last night are keeping him awake. The corvette radioman knocks on the door and enters with an urgent message from naval headquarters in Washington, DC. He hands it to Ramsey.

After reading the message, Ramsey leaves the captain's quarters and rushes to the deck rail. He looks toward the darkened silhouette of the *Beddington*, still lying low in the water. He locates Walker, asleep in the crew's quarters, and touches his shoulder to wake him.

"Harold, I've been directed to go back onboard to assess any chance of salvaging the *Beddington*. I'd like you to go with me at first light, along with Cooper, the engineering officer, and Lewis, the fireman."

At sunrise, the corvette's crew lowers a boat, and the *Beddington* boarding party row out toward the ship, located two hundred yards from the *Ingalls*. They row through some large swells to get there and tie their boat up on the rope ladders the crew had used when they abandoned ship.

The four men climb aboard the low-lying ship on one of those rope ladders hanging over the side. When they reach the deck, Ramsey says, "Harold, take Lewis with you to estimate the amount of water in all compartments and see if it's still pouring in." He tells his engineering officer to do the same in the engine room and to try and locate the bodies of Mathews and Connors. "I want to give those two a proper burial at sea.[4] I'll be on the bridge. After you both finish the surveying the compartments, report to me there."

While Ramsey is on the bridge, he works a combination on the safe there and opens a steel drawer inside, containing the tar sealed top secret package. He places it on the chart table with his logbook and then sits in his swivel chair to log a detailed report about the U-boat attack. Thirty minutes go by before all three men meet with Ramsey on the bridge.

Harold Walker is the first to report. "Sir, this ship will sink soon. The only reason it hasn't so far is because the thick, cork-lined bulkheads in the refrigeration compartments have held out the water. Those compartments are now starting to flood, and all the others are near full."

The engineering officer reports next. "Sir, the engine room is flooded."

"Were you able to find the bodies of Mathews and Connors?"

"Yes, sir. With the help of the others, I was able to get both up on deck. They're each on a board, wrapped in canvas and weighted down with some bricks we found in hold number four. They're ready for your words and their burial at sea."

Harold Walker's warning is directed at Ramsey. "We should hurry to leave the ship. The swells are getting larger, and more water is coming in. I'm not sure we have time for that burial, sir."

Ramsey doesn't answer Walker's concerns. Instead, he takes a Bible from a drawer in the chart table. It's marked with bookmark at a prayer for burial at sea. He grabs the top secret package and

---

[4] *BURIAL AT SEA tradition is an ancient one. The body was slid over the side of a ship after it was wrapped and weighted. Many burials at sea took place in World War II when naval forces operated at sea for months. The prayers of committal have been used by British and U.S. Ships since 1800.*

hurries to the deck where the two bodies await his words before their slide off the boards and into the ocean.

Ramsey starts the prayer of committing the bodies of Mathews and Connors to the sea. "We therefore commit these bodies to the deep,... ".

The prayer is interrupted when a large swell hits the *Beddington* causing a list to port. They slide the bodies overboard and all rush to the rail. The four men climb down the rope ladder. Each man carries a few personal items that had been left behind before when they so hastily abandon ship. Walker holds a picture of his wife; Fireman Lewis, a stack of letters from his mother and his favorite cricket bat. Ramsey pockets his prized meerschaum pipe and carries the black sealed package, marked top secret, under his left arm.

They enter the boat, and, just as they settle in before untying it from the rope ladder, another large swell hits the *Beddington* broadside. Enough ocean water enters to cause the ship to start a rapid plunge, stern first, below the surface. It takes only seven seconds for the ship to complete its disappearance beneath the waves. The boat, with the four men onboard, is caught in the massive suction and drawn down with the ship.

The captain of the *Ingalls* has his binoculars trained on the scene of the *Beddington's* sudden plunge, and he sees the boat with the four men disappear in the boiling surf. He yells to his helmsman, "Jesus! Meaney, the *Beddington* just went down! It took the boarding party boat and the men with it." He points toward the place where the ship sunk. "Get us as close as you can to that bubbling froth and debris field over there."

After, the captain orders a boat lowered to look for survivors, one man is spotted swimming through the swells toward the boat. They haul him in. It's the eighteen-year-old fireman, Paul Lewis. They can locate no other swimmers in the area.

Lewis catches his breath. While shivering and with his eyes tearing, he says, "I made a shallow leaping dive off the bow, but was dragged under anyway. I fought bloody fierce using this as a paddle to get to the surface." Lewis holds up his cricket bat. "After I surfaced, I swam like hell away from that freakin' whirlpool. Tell me, did the officers make it?"

The answer to his question causes Lewis to sob.

The captain of the corvette searches for another hour for the three missing men, but doesn't find them. He sends a sorrowful radio report to naval headquarters. *"Beddington down. . . Ship's Master Ramsey, First Officer Walker, and Engineering Officer Cooper with it . . . Fireman Lewis rescued. . . details follow."*

CHAPTER 14

"Admiral Stone, I called this meeting to brief you on the current situation relative to the U-boat attack on the *Beddington* and *Algonquin*." Ballard looks around the conference table at those seated there. "I've invited General Grove, of the Alsos Mission and the Manhattan Project, along with Under Secretary of the Treasury, John McNeil."

"How many casualties, Ballard?" Admiral Stone asks.

"The *Algonquin* was carrying troops. Eighty-nine went down with the ship, along with fifteen crew members. Sixty-eight survivors were taken to Boston on the *Greenleaf* destroyer. The *Beddington* lost two men when the torpedoes hit and all the rest were rescued by the *Ingalls,* a Canadian corvette. Oh, and five British army guards from the *Beddington* were picked up by a fishing trawler and taken to Provincetown."

Ballard gets a nod from the admiral, and he continues. "Three men, including the ship's master from the *Beddington*, were lost after they returned to their ship by my order to evaluate salvage possibilities." Ballard sighs and pauses before he says, "Their boat was drawn down in the suction caused by the *Beddington's* sudden sinking. One man in that reboarding party survived."

Admiral Stone bows his head for a few seconds after hearing about the loss of men and his commiseration for Ballard's act of ordering the boarding party back on board to an ill-fated death. All in the room join him in a respectful silence. The admiral speaks after a pause of twenty seconds. "The Atlantic war will most likely end soon, and I hope the men that died last night will be the last there is." He directs another question at Admiral Ballard. "Is that top secret package that was to be turned over to Captain Sanders in Boston onboard the Canadian corvette?"

"No, the lone survivor, fireman Paul Lewis from the *Beddington,* said that a black top secret package was carried into the boat by Ramsey, the ship's master, before it went down. It most likely went with him, sir."

"Okay, gentlemen. That package contains a top secret manifest listing the cargo onboard the *Beddington.* Did the captain of the *Ingalls* give you a reading on the ocean depth at the location where the ship sunk, Ballard?"

"Yes, sir. He told me it was approximately four hundred feet."

"General Grove, how does the loss of over one hundred tons of uranium ore affect your Manhattan Project?"

"We need all the uranium ore we can get. Uranium ore, as mined, yields less than one percent in weapons-grade material when processed and enriched. We were, also, extremely interested in that one ton of metalized uranium processed by the Germans that's on board the *Beddington.* It may be close to weapons-grade, and we'd like to know—"

Admiral Stone raises his hands, stopping General Grove's detailed answer. "General, just tell me about the impact on your Manhattan Project?"

"It's not a total loss, admiral. The rest of the Alsos shipment, at nine hundred tons, makes up the majority of uranium ore taken out of Germany. That amount of ore is due to arrive at Oak Ridge in about a week."

"Good, General Grove. How about the US Treasury's loss of platinum and gold on the *Beddington*?" Admiral Stone looks over at John McNeil, the under secretary of the treasury, for the answer.

"That's a large loss, admiral. That shipment was the first payback by the Russians to our Lend-Lease program. It's made up of 2,400 pounds of platinum and 5,670 pounds of gold. That amounts to almost a five million dollar loss at today's prices, sir. Those precious metals could've been used in manufacturing war materials, as well as helping to pay for the war."

Admiral Stone is silent , deep in thought for a moment. Then, he says, "All right, the uranium ore and the precious metals onboard the *Beddington* are lost, as well as the top secret manifest. We do not have the capability for a deep ocean salvage at four hundred feet. I don't want our enemies or other scavengers to salvage that material in the future." With a stern expression and wrinkled brow, Admiral Stone looks straight at Ballard. "These are my orders, Ballard; I want all records of the *Beddington* sinking censured. Contact First Naval Command in Boston and tell them to purge all notations of the *SS Beddington* sinking in their *Eastern Sea Frontier Enemy Action Diary* of 27 and 28 April."

"Shouldn't we, also, brief the survivors and the crews of the warship escorts in convoy XB 32 as to the classified nature of the *Beddington* sinking?" Ballard asks.

"Yes, all those ships are in port at Boston, or they'll soon be there, so you fly to Boston, Ballard, and brief all of the crews and survivors as to the classified status of the *Beddington* sinking. Also, talk to that fishing trawler captain, his crew, and the five British soldiers in Provincetown. Ask for a vow of silence. Tell them that it is in the best interest of the Allied war effort."

"How about the two crew members killed when the *Beddington* was torpedoed and the three that went down with it after it sunk? We have to notify next of kin. It was a British ship, sir."

"Okay, Ballard. Inform the British liaison officer to make notification that those men were transferred to the *Algonquin* and that they went down with it. Add their names to the *Algonquin* casualty list."

"Begging your pardon, sir, but that seems far-fetched."

"Damn it, Ballard, so does all cover-up activity. Get it done!"

Admiral Stone has an afterthought and directs it to Ballard. "Put a top secret letter on file, so all commands in the future will know the classified circumstances related to the sinking of the *Beddington*." The admiral pauses again to gather his thoughts before speaking. "We shall keep the sinking of the *Beddington* under wraps. I'll handle the British and Russian entities through the secretaries of war and state." The admiral stands up from the conference table to make his closing statement.

"Gentlemen, the *SS Beddington* is now a ghost-ship, with its classified cargo and top secret manifest hidden forever at the bottom of the Atlantic Ocean, four hundred feet down."

CHAPTER 15

U-873, Gulf of Maine, May 16, 1945

"Well, Gerhardt. It's finally over. Some of the crew rebelled against our surrender, but they accepted it after I explained that the order to surrender came from their admired Admiral Dönitz, now president of the German Reich. Our U-boat fleet sustained heavy casualties. Heineke told me, in an *enigma* message, that we've lost over seven hundred U-boats and 36,000 crew members during this damn war."

Gerhardt Meyer looks to port and starboard. The destroyer, *Greenleaf*, and a navy tug are shadowing the *U-873* as they head for Portsmouth, New Hampshire. Armed American navy sailors are on deck, at the bow and stern. "What happens next, captain?"

"When we land in Portsmouth, we'll be taken prisoner, but I suppose they'll send us back to Germany soon."

"Yes, Heinz, back to a defeated, bombed-out country without any industry or employment. I guess, we asked for this. Can we re-build our country after the ravages Hitler brought on us? Perhaps, the Americans will be humane conquerors and help us become a strong, peaceable nation."

Captain Haupt gets permission from a navy guard to call down to his navigator below. "Shultz, what's our present position?"

The answer came back to Haupt in degrees longitude and latitude. He takes a note out of his leather jacket breast pocket. Written on it is the position of the SS *Beddington* when his *U-873* torpedoed it. They are now near that spot. Heinz Haupt stares out at the ocean in the general direction of those coordinates while he eyes the note again. "Perhaps, we shall have to help ourselves and our country recover, Gerhardt."

Gerhardt Meyer grins, knowing that his captain has some post-war plan on his mind.

CHAPTER 16

Peter Broderick summons his crew to join him in the trawler's wheelhouse. When Janey Sheffield and Antonio Posada arrive, he says, "We've netted our damned quota. We're heading back to Provincetown. Antonio, make a fresh pot of coffee. You and Janey hang out here while I tell you the latest about that package we netted."

"I called Senator Betty Holloway and told her how the package was confiscated by the navy. She said she'd look into it and that she plans to contact some navy higher-ups at the Pentagon. Also, my lawyer filed a claim with the Government Archives Office in Washington, citing the Freedom of Information Act. Thanks go to your dad, Janey, for suggesting those actions."

Janey takes a sip from her coffee mug. "I've stashed a few haddock and hake samples on ice for my good ole dad to analyze at the Woods Hole lab. They were netted close to the place where the boat's instruments went wacky again."

"Where do we go from here, Pete?" Antonio asks.

"Seems to me that there's something down in the cargo hold of the *Beddington* that the navy wants to keep a deep, dark secret."

"What in hell could be down there that could be so hush-hush, Pete?"

"The answer to that question is probably in the package we netted. It could be the smoking gun."

"The ship may be sitting there, acting as an artificial reef. If that's so, a reef like that would support an ecosystem ranging up the food chain from plankton to whales. What's lurking down there might be hazardous to marine life and harmful to people who eat those fish, Pete."

"Could be, but we'll find out more about that when the fish we netted at the site of the interference are analyzed and when Doctor Sheffield gets his Geiger counter out there to measure that radiated interference. Meanwhile, we'll let Senator Holloway have a go at the navy to declassify the package and wait for my lawyer to do his thing with the Government Archives Office."

"We should pinpoint the exact location of that electronic interference and mark it with a buoy."

"Right, Antonio. I'm in touch with a friend who owns an ocean salvage company out of Portsmouth. I want Sean Kelly to find the *Beddington* and identify it, so we can prove that it exists. If and when he locates that ship and finds out what's down there, then we can make a claim for the wreck. With these frigging fishing quotas the government is hanging on us, we may need a share of any treasure found there to survive. With a share of that treasure, I could buy a larger trawler and fish longer and further out."

Antonio adds his wish for a share of the treasure. "And I could take that trip to Portugal that I've always wanted."

"Whoa! Wait a minute! You said Sean Kelly! Could it be that I dated his son, Brian, in Boston last summer? He graduated from MIT, studied marine biology, and his dad owns a salvage company."

"Brian is working in ocean salvage with his father, Janey."

"Hope we'll meet again. He's the best."

"When are you going to visit your great-aunt, Pete, and find out what she knows about the *Beddington* sinking?"

"Soon after we dock, I'll be off to Aunt Annie's house in Chatham."

CHAPTER 17

After the *Elizabeth Ann lll* docks at Provincetown and the catch is off- loaded, Peter Broderick drives to Chatham. He walks up the flagstone path of a gray shingled, two-story house, carrying a cooler in his left hand. When he gets to the door, he knocks twice. His great-aunt Annie Broderick opens the door right away, as if she's been waiting there since he'd called her two hours before.

"Oh, Peter! It has been such a long time."

He hugs her and talks into her ear while doing so. "I know, Aunt Annie. Been spending a lot of time on the boat, but I'm here now and brought your favorite. Take a look."

Peter opens the cooler, and the spry, eighty-six-year-old spinster peeks in at a six pound halibut, all cleaned and ready for the oven.

"Oh, my!" She shakes her silver-topped head. "I haven't had halibut in so long. Thank you! Thank you, Peter! Come! Sit in the kitchen while I fix my special sauce and get this beauty in the oven. I have some fresh asparagus and those small potatoes you like. They'll go nicely with the fish."

Peter sits at the kitchen table, sipping a chilled glass of Chablis while they chat. "I thought you were going to sell this house and move to that assisted living place over in Falmouth."

"I thought about that, but I'm still active. I love this house. I visit with my friends—what's left of them—and walk to Main Street most days. I have lunch and browse in the *Yellow Umbrella Bookstore.* I was given a tour of that assisted living place over in

Falmouth, and it's nice, but there were too many old people milling around. They didn't seem to do anything but wait for breakfast, lunch, and dinner, and for the evening bingo games to start."

Peter laughs at her description of the old people at the assisted living place. "Do you remember as far back as 1945 during the Second World War? I have a few things to ask you about it."

"Oh, my! Let's see. I lived in Provincetown then, while my father, your great-grandfather, went out fishing on the first *Elizabeth Ann*. The war years were sad for so many, but they were exciting for a girl of eighteen. There were navy and coast guard men all over the place."

"When I was a kid, Aunt Annie, you told me about your dad rescuing survivors from a ship that was sunk by a German U-boat."

"I did? I must've had more than one glass of Chablis at the time. The sinking of that ship was supposed to be kept a secret. In fact, we had a visit from the navy, and they made my dad, his crew, and the survivors take a vow of silence about that."

"Well, I netted a package out in the Gulf of Maine with some lettering on it. The words written there were *SS Beddington* and *top secret*. A navy guy took it away from me."

"Yes. The *Beddington*. I do recall that name. That was the ship Dad rescued the survivors from."

"Can you tell me more about those survivors and that vow of silence?"

"Should I, Peter? Perhaps, I shouldn't have told you about it back then."

"I need all the information I can get to prove that that ship was sunk. We think the navy, back in 1945, covered it up and is still doing so, sixty-eight years later."

"Why do you care?"

"There may be something in the *Beddington* cargo that's dangerous to marine life. I'm working on getting that package we netted back from the navy. I think it will tell us what's down there."

"Oh, my! Well, if you say it's okay, I'll help in any way I can."

"It's okay, Aunt Annie. Now, tell me all you can remember about the *Beddington* sinking."

"Well, I remember things that happened back in 1945 much better than where I put my reading glasses two hours ago. The five British army survivors stayed at our house in Provincetown for three days until their sergeant could arrange billets for the five at Camp Edwards in Falmouth."

"Is that where the navy came to ask the five British guys and my great-grandfather for a vow of silence?"

"Yes! Oh, and I must tell you." A blush came to her face. "I fell head over heels for one of those soldiers. He was my age, at eighteen. Yes, Private Jimmy Lawson was my first love, and I'd venture to say that he became my last. Jimmy stayed on Cape Cod, at Camp Edwards, for three months before returning to England. We dated—movies, picnics on the beach, and trips to Boston."

"Did you keep in touch?"

"Oh, yes. Love letters for over two years. He planned to visit and wrote to me about us getting married. In those days, it wasn't like today. I couldn't just jump on a plane and cross the ocean on a whim. When Jimmy married an English girl in 1952, it broke my heart. It has been only Christmas and birthday cards every year since."

"Is this Jimmy Lawson still living in England?"

"As far as I know. I received a Christmas card last year. He's eighty-six years old, and his wife died two years ago."

"Do you have his address and phone number?"

"Yes, I do, but I've never called him. And, Peter, I have something in the attic that might help you prove that the *Beddington* sunk."

"What's up there?"

"My father saved all his *Elizabeth Ann* logbooks. I must have the one from 1945."

CHAPTER 18

Captain Pete and his mate, Antonio Posada, are preparing the trawler *Elizabeth Ann lll* for another fishing trip. They fill the fuel tanks and load ice before leaving Provincetown Harbor for the Gulf of Maine.

"How did it go with your aunt, Pete?"

"Aunt Annie was reluctant to tell me much at first. She still held on to that patriotic vow of silence she took back in 1945. After a while, she changed her mind, though."

"How come?"

"I explained that we needed to prove that the *Beddington* was sunk before we can get that package we netted back from the navy. Aunt Annie, being a fishermen's daughter, was sensitive to the possibility that radiation from the ship's cargo might harm marine life."

"Do you think the package will tell us what's down there, Pete?"

"I do."

"What did she remember about the *Beddington*?"

"She recalled the *SS Beddington* sinking, as told by her father, and the five British army survivors being picked up by him and brought to her house. In fact, she fell in love with one of those survivors. He's still alive, living in England."

"You should contact him to get more proof of that sinking. Hurry! He must be pretty old."

"He's eighty-six, Antonio. I plan on calling him before we leave port today, at about 2:00 p.m. his time. Speaking of more proof, Antonio, look what I found in my aunt Annie's attic." Pete reaches into a drawer in the chart table and takes out an *Elizabeth Ann* log-book dated 1945.

"Wow! That's a find."

"Yeah, she dug it out from an old sea chest."

Janey Sheffield came onboard. "Sorry I'm late...damn tourist traffic on Route Six."

"Hey! You're just in time to get a look at this."

"What have you got?"

"The *Elizabeth Ann* logbook from 1945."

Pete flips to a page dated April 27, 1945 and reads it to Janey and Antonio.

"*1920 hours...observed smoke on the horizon...proceeded near its location... two ships torpedoed by German U-boat...picked up five British army survivors from SS Beddington...stood by until relieved by radio message from Canadian corvette, Ingalls...headed to P-town with five survivors onboard.*"

Pete turns to the next page in the logbook and reads:

"*April 28...1610 hours...got visit from two navy officers at home... briefing to keep secret for war effort...took vow of silence pledge, with survivors, not to mention sinking of the Beddington.*"

"Wow! This really proves the navy didn't want anyone to know that that ship was sunk...either back then or now!" Antonio exclaims. Then, he asks his usual question. "Where do we go from here, Pete?"

"Sean Kelly, the salvage guy, will do the search with side-scan sonar devices around the area where we netted the package and got that interference with our instruments. When he finds the *Beddington*, he'll talk salvage and sharing possibilities with us."

"What's Sean Kelly like? I hope he's something like his son. We became fast friends, and I'd guess even more than that."

"Sean's a piece of work, Janey. He's a diamond in the rough from County Cork, Ireland. He found gold and silver cargo on a ship sunk by the Germans in the Irish Sea during World War Two. He salvaged it, made big bucks, and moved his outfit to Portsmouth, New Hampshire. He's been working out of there for five years and has found and salvaged more sunken treasure around here."

"Can't wait to meet him and see his son again. When is Captain Kelly going to start this search?"

"Next Monday morning, Janey. The search could take a couple of days or more."

"We'll be back in port by then. Do you think I could go out with them?"

"I'll call Sean and ask him. If he says it's okay for you to join him on the *Deep Adventure*, you can board the boat in Portsmouth. But watch out, he can be gruff at times."

"Good. I hope he says yes. I can handle gruff. Have you heard anything from Senator Holloway?"

"She'll meet with some navy brass at the Pentagon with proof of the ship's existence if Sean Kelly locates the *Beddington*. How about Doctor Sheffield's lab analysis of the radiation level in the fish we froze and sent him?"

"My dad will have those fish samples analyzed by the time we return from this trip. He plans on making some Geiger counter readings there when and if Kelly locates the *Beddington*. He'll tell us the results of both tests at the same time."

"Good. We'll need his input when the senator meets with the navy. By the way, my lawyer struck out in his try to release our package from the naval archives in Washington."

* * *

"Hello. Is this James Lawson?"
"Yes. Who's calling, please?"

"I'm Peter Broderick, the great-nephew of Annie Broderick and the great-grandson of the *Elizabeth Ann*'s captain. I'm calling from Cape Cod."

There's a pause before Jimmy speaks. "Is she all right?"

"Yes, she's fine."

"That's grand. I've not forgotten her. I may get to America soon, and the first thing I'll do is knock her up."

Peter is stunned for a moment by that English expression. "Sir, you mean you'll look her up?"

Jimmy chuckles. "I'm sorry. That has American slang connotations. Of course, as you say, I do mean that I'll look her up."

After the vision of his eighty-six-year-old Aunt Annie wearing maternity clothes fades away, Peter laughs. "Thanks for your explanation, Jimmy."

"Righto, and what may I do for you, Peter?"

"You're a survivor of the *SS Beddington* that was sunk by a U-boat near Cape Cod in 1945, right?"

"Righto, it was Annie's father who rescued me and four other mates. I did take a vow of silence then, but, after almost seventy years, I'd guess I can confirm that incident for you. The five of us were guarding a secret cargo on that ship. We had no idea what it was."

"Did you see the *Beddington* sink?"

"No, the ship's master—bless him—ordered all the compartments buttoned so tight that it didn't sink until the next morning. I met some of the *Beddington* crew in Boston later on. Those lads were onboard the corvette *Ingalls*, and they watched her go down with the boarding crew, which included Ramsey, the ship's master. Those survivors, also, took that vow of silence about its sinking."

"Mr. Lawson, we believe that the sunken cargo on that ship could be dangerous to our marine life. Our navy still refuses to admit the *Beddington* was sunk. We need to prove that it was and find out what's down there in its cargo. There's a package I netted from my trawler that may give us that answer, but the navy confiscated that package, and we are trying to get it back from them."

"I see. How may I assist you in that endeavor?"

"Could you send a sworn statement to me, telling all you know about the *Beddington* sinking, your vow of silence, that secret cargo, and your rescue?"

"Yes, I shall do that. I'll contact my barrister and request that he notarize the document I send you."

After Peter provides his post office address, he says, "Thank you for your help, Mr. Lawson."

"It's my pleasure to assist the great-nephew of Annie and the great-grandson of the kind man who rescued me. Please pass on my regards to your aunt and tell her I may soon visit her."

"I will, sir, and good-bye."

"Cheerio, Peter."

CHAPTER 19

Janey Sheffield finds the *Deep Adventure* in Portsmouth Harbor docked among several other boats. It's easy for her to identify because it's larger than all of the others. It has a green shamrock painted on the wheelhouse bulkhead and an Irish flag flies next to the American one high up on its mast. She walks up the gangplank and discovers there's no one on deck.

Janey sets her backpack down and shouts "hello" three times, each one louder than the last, until a muffled response comes from below deck.

"I hear ye, lass. Keep your knickers on while I finish oiling this engine."

Five minutes pass before a hatch on deck is pushed aside and a head appears adorned with bright red hair and a handlebar mustache of the same color. The rest of six-foot-three Sean Kelly rises up through the hatch. He wipes his hands with a rag, tweaks the end of his mustache, and asks, "Can ye cook, lass?"

Captain Pete's warning about Kelly's gruffness helps with her fast response. She tosses her single blonde pigtail over her right shoulder and answers, "I can make an Irish stew that'll knock your socks off."

Kelly's weathered face crinkles into a grin. "Good on ye, lass. I booted our combination cook and deckhand off the boat yesterday. He burnt the bacon and had the gall to serve it. I'll take you to the galley and your quarters. After, my proverbial son, whom you've met, will show you around the rest of this ship."

Janey checks out the well-equipped galley. She finds a microwave and a four-burner stove with stainless steel pots and pans above the grill. There's a stainless steel table in the dining area that seats twelve. After inspecting the galley, she leaves her backpack on the bunk in her room, and Kelly leads her to the door of the *remote operated vehicle* (ROV) control module on the main deck.

"I'll be leaving you here, Janey. Just go in there and find Brian. He's looking over the shoulder of our ROV pilot, trying to learn the program and how to control an ROV without dumping the awkward bastard on the ocean floor."

She opens the door to the ROV control module. It's dark except for the luminescent glow given off by the computer displays mounted on all four walls. As soon as her eyes adapt to the luminous scene, she becomes aware of Brian Kelly standing near her. She notes that his red hair is shades darker than the flaming red of his dad's.

"Hi, Janey. Hey, I wanted to get in touch with you again, but my finals came, and, after that, my dad needed me here, but—"

Janey interrupts him. She puts her right hand on his shoulder. "Brian, I was locked in my dorm room for days and days with only bread and water to survive on while waiting for your call or text."

He laughs. "I'll bet you were. Anyway, you're here now, and we'll go out and try to find that ship. I'll show you around. Where do you want to start?"

"This ROV control room looks like the best place."

"I'm still learning how to pilot an ROV, but I'll introduce you to our expert ROV pilot." Brian leads her over to a guy bent low over a console.

"Janey, meet Kevin Fortuna."

A tall, dark-haired man with a full beard gets up from his seat, turns, and takes her hand. "Hi! I'll give you the Cook's tour."

"I am the ship's cook."

"Did our captain recruit you or enslave you?"

"A little of both."

"Okay, I like my eggs over easy with link sausage." He points to the console in front. "This display will show acoustic images of what the two side-scan sonar devices will see on the ocean bottom. The *Deep Adventure* will tow a side-scan sonar device on both sides of the ship."

"Can those towed sonar devices show detail, like a name painted on a ship?"

"No, it just shows the profile of an object's mass, like a ship on the bottom."

"How do you get detail like that?"

"We use the *Super Mohawk* ROV to get comprehensive pictures of an image like that lettering of a ship's name." Kevin moves to another console.

"How do you control the *Super Mohawk*?"

"The *Super Mohawk* has vertical and horizontal thrusters to move it toward an objective. Cameras and bright LED lights at six thousand lumens each are mounted on it, and I control the ROV by moving these joysticks. That sends command signals to the thrusters and cameras through an analog umbilical cord."

"Where can I see that detail?"

Kevin points to a screen above the console. "The *Super Mohawk's* position and its photos are shown in real time on this display."

"Kevin, what about salvaging objects inside or around a ship with an ROV?"

"The *Super Mohawk* ROV is capable of a deep dive with an umbilical cord hook-up." Kevin moves across the room to another console. "As I mentioned before, the ROV is controlled by thrusters I turn on and off with these two joysticks on this control box. I do this while looking at the ROV on this engineering screen."

"Can it pick up things?"

"Yeah, it's designed to pick up objects weighing as much as seventy pounds with manipulator arms and jaws. It can place them in a steel box where our stabilized two hundred ton deck crane can do the heavy lifting to get the items in the box on board the ship. Is that enough until we deploy the ROV?"

"Yes, that'll do it for now. Thanks, Kevin."

"When we get on site, I'll show you the real world activity of this ROV." Kevin chuckles. "After you prepare our meals, of course."

Brian takes Janey on a bow to stern tour of the 260 foot *Deep Adventure*. He introduces her to the rest of its eight-man crew. She takes in all the cranes, ROVs, nets, pulleys, and reels of cable used in deep salvage. In the bridge, there's high tech, navigational aids, including a ship and crane stabilization system.

When they finish the ship's tour, she asks, "When do we leave port, Brian? I'm eager to locate that ship and find out what's down there."

"We leave tomorrow morning at high tide, around six. We'll be on site by noon."

"I suppose that means I'll be cooking breakfast at five in the morning."

"It does...and please don't burn the bacon. I'd like you to stay onboard for a while. Hey! Tell me more about that radiation encounter, and your concerns with the ecosystem around that ship we're going to locate. I did a paper at MIT on the Japanese tsunami nuclear reactor meltdown and its impact on marine life."

"Take me to your favorite Portsmouth pub, Brian, and I'll tell all I know over a cold, tall draft of that local brew, Smuttynose."

"Okay, that'll work. I have to go ashore to get grub for the cook."

Janey smiles. "The cook will be in the galley at five tomorrow morning when you start your prep there...my sous chef."

CHAPTER 20

"Okay, two more passes with the side-scan sonar, and I'm outta here. We've made twelve passes around the location Pete Broderick gave me."

That brusque message from the bridge by Sean Kelly came through the speaker in the ROV control room. Janey and Brian are bent over the sonar display where Kevin Fortuna sits when they hear that order from Kelly.

"This will be the thirteenth sonar pass," Kevin says. "Is anyone superstitious?"

"I'm not. Thirteen is my dad's lucky number," Janey answers.

Tension peaks in the ROV control room. Kevin rubs his beard, and Brian has beads of sweat on his forehead, even though the room temperature is controlled to sixty-eight degrees. Janey fiddles with her pony tail while they all stare at the display, showing sonar images on the ocean floor, four hundred feet below.

They are interrupted by Captain Sean Kelly's booming voice blaring out of the speaker again. "For fuck's sake! Most of my instrumentation here has gone crazy. Radar is all white noise. VHF radio is screaming like a freakin' banshee!"

Janey grabs a handheld transmitter. "Captain, stop the ship. This is the same interference we got on the *Elizabeth Ann*. I think we're near the *Beddington*."

Kevin takes the mike away from her. "Janey, he can't stop the ship with the side-scan sonar being towed. If he did that, the sonars would sink to the ocean bottom, and we'd lose them."

Kevin clicks the mike button and speaks to Captain Kelly. "Sean, continue on your heading at the same speed and then come around to a position 180 from it. I'll confirm the data and get a good image if there's a wreck down there."

Captain Sean Kelly answers, "Will do, but, if you come up without a ship wreck, I'm outta here."

Twenty minutes go by before Kevin blurts out, "Bingo! I've got an image that looks like a ship on its side." He's busy focusing in, determining its exact location and recording that information.

Janey and Brian see a large hulk on the screen that does look like a ship. Janey yells out one word that tells of her elation: "Awesome!"

They celebrate with high fives that soon advance to hugs all around.

Their celebration is interrupted by another roar from the speaker. "When can I move the freakin' ship away from this interference?"

Kevin answers, "Captain, we would like to deploy the *Super Mohawk* ROV to get some detailed pictures of the wreck."

"Okay, but hurry up and get it done. I don't want my instruments jumping around again like they've leprechauns dancing inside them. By the way, Kevin, why didn't your side-scan sonar get bothered the same way my electronic stuff in this wheelhouse did?"

"My guess is that the frequency of the side-scan sonar is too low to be interfered with by the kind of high frequency radiation coming from around that ship."

"Okay, smart-ass ROV pilot. Get on with deploying the *Super Mohawk.*"

* * *

Two hours later, the *Super Mohawk* ROV approaches the sonar target of a wreck that could be the *SS Beddington*. Janey and Brian have intense, wide-eyed expressions on their faces as they look over Kevin's shoulder. The display they're watching shows details that resemble a ship with a debris field surrounding it.

Janey releases a breath she'd held for over ten seconds. "Look, there are a couple of portholes over there, Kevin." She points to a place on the screen. "And see all those broken wooden barrels next to the ship?"

"Yeah, some of the cargo may have been dumped out of its hold when she hit bottom. Looks like the ship may have broken in two. I wouldn't expect to see so many smashed up barrels, though."

"And look at all those fish swimming around the ship. Looks like that artificial reef is supporting all kinds of marine life. This is amazing!" Brian adds.

"I can see the ship's bow. Could you move the *Super Mohawk* in closer, Kevin? There's some bleary red lettering right there." She points to a place on the display.

"Hold on a minute. I can adjust the optics and lights here for a clearer picture of those letters. I'll activate the high pressure water jets on the ROV to clear the silt around them. "

A close up image of the lettering on the bow comes up on the screen:SS BEDDINGTON

Kevin, then, moves the ROV along the side of the ship until the stern is reached. The ROV closes in on some letters there.

SS BEDDINGTON

AVONMOUTH ENGLAND

Janey yells out, "Awesome! Now, we have the proof to show the navy that this ship really exists. If we get the package back from them, it may tell us what's radiating in the cargo of the *Beddington* that's causing interference to a ship's instruments and could be harmful to marine life."

Kevin relinquishes his seat and the joystick controlling the *Super Mohawk* to Brian. Then, Kevin says, "Make a few passes around the ship with the ROV and record what it sees down there. It will be a good experience for you, and we'll need that data when we salvage. I'll be close by in case you get into trouble."

When data from the ROV is recorded and a small coded beacon buoy anchored and deployed on the surface, Captain Kelly provides Janey with a handheld transmitter.

"Here. This transmitter is coded to match the beacon buoy's receiver. That buoy is anchored on the bottom at the *Beddington's* location. Your dad can use it to find the *Beddington* when he runs his Geiger counter radiation tests."

* * *

Janey places a call to Peter Broderick. "Guess what I've got, Pete?"

"What've you got, Janey?"

"I've got photographic proof that the *SS Beddington* exists four-hundred feet at the bottom of the Atlantic."

"No kidding? That's great news. Put Sean Kelly on. I want to thank him and talk about salvage possibilities. We'll celebrate when you get back."

"We're celebrating now on the way into Portsmouth, Pete. I cooked an Irish stew and acquired a taste for Guinness, and Sean Kelly taught me how to step dance."

* * *

As the *Deep Adventure* heads for Portsmouth, Janey and Brian stand at the bow and watch the lights of the city come into their view. When the ship enters the harbor, the reflection from city lights casts a gold and platinum hue on the water's surface.

"I read some World War Two history telling about five German U-boats captured in the Atlantic by the navy in May 1945 and escorted to Portsmouth Harbor." Brian points to the gray walls of a large island prison to the right. "The German U-boat crews were detained over there."

"Brian, I wonder if the U-boat that torpedoed the *SS Beddington* was one of those captured."

"It could've been...since the *Beddington* was torpedoed and sunk in April 1945 close to the time those U-boats were captured and the crews interned in that prison. Our *Beddington* salvage venture may solve that mystery and others surrounding the ship. I'm looking forward to recovering cargo from that ship and finding what's causing that mysterious radiated interference my dad and you saw."

"I'd like to be in on any salvage of the *Beddington* operation on-board the *Deep Adventure*. Can you make that happen?"

"You're in, Janey."

"I thought you might need a cook."

"What else would we want you along for? Let's see...you're a marine biologist; you love the ocean and its marine life, and you want it protected. Besides all that, I like having you around."

"Also, I've got an awesome pair of sea legs."

"I've noticed. I'll call or text you when my dad and Peter Broderick get the salvage operation put together."

"Until you call, my cell phone will never leave my hand."

Their kiss isn't a long one, but it is a good one, lasting until Captain Kelly blows the ship's loud fog horn on purpose.

CHAPTER 21

US Senator Holloway's Boston office, August 12, 2013.

"Senator Holloway, I'll introduce you to the group sitting around this table."

"Do that, Captain Broderick, but I already know this gentleman." She smiles and nods toward Doctor Jay Sheffield. "We've worked together before on fishery issues that affect this state. Hello, Jay."

"This is his daughter, Janey Sheffield. She graduated from Northeastern with a degree in marine biology. She works on my boat. Next to her is Sean Kelly, captain of the *Deep Adventure*, a salvage ship. And beside Sean is his son, Brian, a graduate of MIT, also, in marine biology. He works on his dad's ship."

"Welcome, all. We are here to discuss an approach to the navy, as well as other government entities like the Environmental Protection Agency (EPA). It's about getting our hands on the package confiscated by the navy after it was netted by Captain Broderick's trawler. If you'll all bear with me, I have some questions to ask of Doctor Sheffield."

"Why is this package so important, Jay?"

"I recently performed Geiger counter measurements in and around the wreck of the *Beddington*. I think that package may define the source of the high levels of gamma radiation I measured."

"I don't know a thing about gamma radiation or any other radiation effect, for that matter. What's the bottom line?"

"Senator, the level of gamma radiation I measured can pass through a person's skin. If one were standing next to the source of that radiation for an hour, he or she would die."

"You don't say! Is it dangerous to people on the surface, like in a ship?"

"No, its source is down four hundred feet. It's attenuated by seawater and not hazardous to anyone on the surface. However, it can create electronic interference when its high radio frequency is amplified by the receivers of ships passing above it. This type of interference has been observed on instrumentation by myself as well as Captains Kelly and Broderick."

"How far does this high level of gamma radiation extend?"

"Fortunately, its source is from a twelve by twelve foot area near the shipwreck."

"Is that same radiation a hazard to fish in the area of the ship?"

"Over the years, since it was sunk, the *Beddington* has become an artificial reef inhabited by marine life, senator. I've completed a study of some fish samples netted from near the wreck."

"And, what was the outcome?"

"My spectrum analysis study at the lab in Woods Hole shows high levels of radioactive iodine and cesium in the fish I sampled."

"Without getting into numbers I won't understand, how does what you measured in the fish at Woods Hole lab compare with the radiation levels in fish measured by the Japanese after the tsunami caused their reactor to melt down?"

"Not quite as high, but approaching the same levels."

"Okay, that's enough. Here's what I need. Jay, put together a presentation showing your Geiger counter measurements and fish analysis readings. Captain Kelly, I need your documented proof of the *Beddington* find. I assume you have a video recording showing this, right?

"I do, and I have the precise location of the wreck that I may not divulge to anyone until my claim is final."

"Good. Be ready to be in Washington at the Pentagon's naval headquarters next Monday morning at ten with your video. I'd, also, like you there in case questions come up on how to safely recover whatever's causing that radiation. Captain Broderick, I need you to come along with your great-grandfather's 1945 logbook. You have that proof of the *Beddington* sinking to show the navy. Also, bring along the affidavit by the British survivor from that ship."

"How about Brian Kelly and Janey Sheffield, senator? They may come in handy if questions on the hazard to marine life come up. Brian wrote a paper at MIT on the radiation levels in fish after the tsunami reactor meltdown."

"Of course, bring them along. Peter Broderick, we're going to kick some navy butt and get your package back for you."

CHAPTER 22

Pentagon, Washington, DC, August 19, 2013

"Alright, gentlemen and ladies of the interested parties, you've seen the documented proof that the *SS Beddington* was sunk by a German U-boat in 1945." Senator Holloway addresses the meeting with that statement and continues. "Further, that ship lies on the ocean bottom in the Gulf of Maine, emitting a dangerous level of radiation from its cargo. Any questions?"

Ann Wilson of the Environmental Protection Agency says, "Senator Holloway, I believe the first order of business is to stop all fishing in the area surrounding that ship. Doctor Sheffield, how large an area?"

"I've put some thought into this. I believe that an ocean area of five square nautical miles surrounding the *Beddington* would be sufficient initially. I'll continue to sample fish inside and outside of that area for levels of radioactive cesium and iodine to see if that proposed limit is sufficient."

"Okay, doctor. I'll get that ban imposed immediately. Now, how about getting at the source of that radiation and removing it?"

"That's a salvage job that Captain Kelly can address, Mrs. Wilson," Sheffield adds. "But before that task is started, it would be nice to know more about what's down there in the *Beddington* cargo, causing high gamma radiation. The package we're here to recover could tell us that"

Al Chabot of the Food and Drugs Agency asks, "What about the immediate danger to those who eat fish caught near that location?"

Peter Broderick responds, "Sir, I have put the catch my trawler netted near the ship in cold storage until more is known about the level of dangerous radiation effect to anyone eating those fish. Brian Kelly, do you have anything to add?"

"I wrote a paper while at MIT on the impact on fish in the area of that meltdown in Japan caused by the tsunami. For what it's worth, estimates by some Japanese scientists may have been skewed, but they've stated that radioactive cesium and iodine levels found in fish from seawater near that disaster would not be dangerous to a person unless over twenty-five pounds were consumed in a year," Brian adds.

"That does not give me a warm feeling, Mr. Kelly," Al Chabot says. "The Japanese were inconsistent with their estimates after that meltdown. Food and Drug will attempt to set a safely measured level for fish caught in an area five nautical miles around that wreck. Can someone here tell me how many other fishing vessel have caught fish in those waters?"

Captain Parmenter of the Coast Guard answers, "Captain Broderick and Doctor Sheffield notified the Coast Guard about the problem. We are, at present, active in reviewing logbooks from all commercial fishing boats working in New England waters. We'll find out if they've caught fish in the five nautical mile area prescribed by Doctor Sheffield."

"Admiral Jordan, we are led to believe that the top secret package netted by Captain Broderick may include a manifest that will tell us the source of that dangerous radiation. I represent those fishing in the waters near the *Beddington* and many fish-eating constituents. I need to have that package now. I don't want to engage a senate investigative committee to get it, but I will if necessary."

"Senator, I've looked into this situation and found a letter that was filed back in 1945, justifying the top secret classification of that package. And, as a matter of fact, the package does contain the manifested cargo of the *Beddington*."

"Was the taking of that package from Peter Broderick by the navy an appropriate action, Admiral Jordan?"

"Senator, it was proper to cover-up the sinking of the *Beddington* at the time, over sixty-eight years ago, during World War Two, because of the nature of its cargo."

"Could you elaborate on that reasoning, admiral? What was so secret about that cargo?"

"It was uranium ore and metalized uranium ingots taken from Germany along with precious metals as part of the Russians' Lend-Lease payback, Senator Holloway."

"Why was there such a secret cover-up over that ship being sunk, admiral?"

"We did not have deep salvage capability at the time, and the navy didn't want any other country to salvage the uranium ore."

"Did other countries, at the time, have deep salvage capability?"

"We weren't sure of that, senator, but we did know then that, following the Hiroshima and Nagasaki A-bombings, many other countries would be interested in acquiring an atomic bomb, and, to do that, they needed a large supply of uranium ore. That large supply of uranium ore was contained in the *Beddington* cargo. Also, that metalized uranium would be an interesting find to the world scientists. We had no idea the Germans were so close to making an atomic bomb."

"Wasn't the attraction of those precious metals in the cargo a factor that would've brought keen interest from any salvager, Admiral Jordan?"

"Yes, the Russian Lend-Lease payback of precious metals in the cargo would've brought salvagers to the ship and, hence, the uranium. The decision at the time was to make the *Beddington* nonexistent or, if you will, a ghost-ship."

"Should the *Beddington* incident still be top secret after sixty-eight years, admiral?"

"Senator, Commander Burrows, that First Naval District officer who confiscated the top secret package from Captain Broderick reacted only to the classification issue. He should have done more research into the why and wherefor of that classification. There's a letter on file at Naval Archives detailing the facts behind the *Beddington* incident. By the way, the uranium onboard the *Beddington* was part of that captured in Germany by some brave troops and scientists during their Alsos Mission in 1945."

"If I may, admiral, uranium ore as mined will not emit the level of radiation I saw coming from near the *Beddington*. There's something else down there. Could I take a look at the manifest?"

"Yes, you may, Doctor Sheffield. I've had it declassified." The admiral speaks to an aide. "Charlie, go get that damned package."

The admiral's aide returns to the conference room, carrying a black, tar-covered, oilskin package that'd been split open by applying a heat source.

"Captain Broderick, is this the package your trawler netted?"

Peter Broderick stands up and looks it over. "Yes, it is, senator. One in the same."

"Whoa! Has the navy checked that package for any radiation contamination?" Doctor Sheffield asks.

"Yes, we did, and it came up negative," the admiral's aide, Commander Charles Parker, says.

"How far away from the interference did your trawler net this package, Pete?" Sheffield asks.

"About five nautical miles."

"I might add, Doctor Sheffield. A top secret package would be secured in the ship's safe as normal shipboard security procedure." The admiral, then, says, "This would keep it away from any contamination by a radiation source."

"So, it didn't go down with the ship?" Doctor Sheffield asks.

"No, according to the letter filed in 1945 about the *Beddington* incident, that package was in the hands of the ship's master, not onboard the ship when it sunk. The package was presumed to be carried down with him when the boarding party boat was sucked under near the *Beddington*. This is based on the report of Fireman Paul Lewis. He was the boarding party's sole survivor. This is stated in that same letter on file."

"Admiral, may Captain Broderick take custody of this package as the rightful owner?"

"Yes, he may, senator."

"Before you leave, Captain Kelly, I'd like to schedule a meeting with you to discuss the salvaging of whatever is causing that radiation." Ann Wilson of the Environmental Protection Agency asks, "Would tomorrow at ten be okay? Of course, this effort would be accomplished before any attempt on your part to salvage those precious metals. I assume you will make an immediate claim for the wreck."

CHAPTER 23

Peter Broderick, with the package held under his arm, Sean and Brian Kelly, and Jay and Janey Sheffield leave the meeting and the Pentagon after thanking Rear Admiral Roscoe Jordan, Senator Betty Holloway, and the other meeting attendees.

On the way out, Sean Kelly makes a request. "After sitting in that meeting for three hours, my mouth feels as dry as winter heather. I know a pub nearby where there's Guinness on tap. Let's have a look at the manifest there."

They enter the Red Lion Pub and are seated at a table.

"Can we look at the manifest right now, Pete?" Janey asks.

"Even before we order the Guinness? That's blasphemy, lass," Sean Kelly exclaims, while mocking an expression of shock.

They're all so eager to read the manifest that it takes precedence over their Guinness libation. Peter Broderick opens the slit in the black package. He removes the manifest and places it on the table. They all begin to read.

* * *

CARGO MANIFEST SS BEDDINGTON
(Top Secret Eyes only)
Sailing April 18, 1945—Avonmouth to Boston via Halifax

ITEM	WEIGHT	LOCATION
495 barrels uranium ore	approx. 100 tons	Holds # 1&2
5 Barrels metalized ingots	I ton	Hold # 3
160 ingots of platinum	2400 LBS	Hold # 4
210 ingots of gold	5670 LBS	Hold # 4

* * *

"Jesus, Mary, and Joseph! That gold alone at today's market price is $1,288 an ounce." After saying that, Sean Kelly takes out his pocket calculator, and his fingers tap a few numbers. He shows the figure on his calculator to all at the table. It's $116,847,360.

"That is amazing. Around $117,000,000 in gold alone? But let's not lose sight of the first order of business—bringing up to the surface that source of radiation," Jay Sheffield says. "I'm interested to know more about the item on the manifest stated as 'one ton of metalized uranium ingots.' Sounds like some material that was processed by the Germans well beyond uranium ore."

"Wait! There's another paper besides the manifest folded and tucked down deep in the package." Janey hands her find to Sean Kelly.

"Glory be to the sea! This is just what I need to study the *Beddington's* layout before I start the salvage operation. It's a diagram made by the ship builder showing all the compartments and holds."

"Why would that be in the package with the manifest?" Janey asks.

"We'll never know for sure, lass. Perhaps, the hold location of the top secret cargo was also top secret," Sean speculates.

CHAPTER 24

Back from Washington, DC, Captain Sean Kelly and his son Brian stop by Provincetown on their way to Portsmouth. They join Pete, Antonio, and Janey onboard the *Elizabeth Ann lll.*

"How did your meeting with the EPA go, Sean?" Pete asks.

"A lot went down. The Environmental Protection Agency was joined by a bevy of other agencies—Food and Drug, State Department, FEMA, Homeland Security, and some CIA spooks."

"Bottom line, Sean, did you get the salvage job?"

"After a four hour meeting, I received a cost plus contract to salvage that one ton of metalized uranium ingots that Doctor Sheffield believes is the source of his high gamma radiation readings."

"How about all that uranium ore on the *Beddington?*" Janey asks.

"The experts say it's not hazardous. They believe that the uranium ore, as mined, will harmlessly return to the earth where it came from. We'll leave it be."

"Did you claim the wreck?" Pete asks.

Sean Kelly tweaks his red handlebar mustache with his left hand. "Yes, but, before I proceeded, I wanted to make sure that every Ivan, Nigel, and Harry didn't tie up the claim with a counterclaim. Turns out that, since the *Beddington* sinking was a deep cover up back in 1945, all evidence of that ship's existence was hidden by the Brits and the Russians. Back in the day, that deception was controlled by the US State Department. So, there's no justification for any other claim coming at me."

"Was the *Beddington* insured?" Pete asks.

"Probably, but, according to Lloyd's of London, there are no records there on the *Beddington*. The insurance policies were most likely destroyed as part of that cover-up."

"So, the wreck of the Beddington is yours, Sean."

"Yeah, Pete, my marine lawyer, Jonathan Fryer, is handling all the details. He will submit legal notices in thirty-five American newspapers asking if others will make claim to the *Beddington* wreck. That's just a formality. Fryer is the best. He'll also sort out any other issues, such as anything coming forth from federal or state interests about their claim to the wreck of a ship that never was."

"So, where do we go from here, Captain Kelly?" Antonio Posada asks.

"Phase one of the salvage will be to bring up the metalized uranium ingots. This will be done robotically. The EPA will provide three men for the handling of the radioactive material. They'll be responsible for sealing the uranium ingots in steel barrels lined with lead and all involved will be wearing protective clothing."

"Will anybody in our crew have to handle those ingots, Dad?"

"Not really, Brian. The large and small crane operators will wear protective clothing, and the rest of the crew won't be allowed near the salvage operation. Everyone on board will wear radiation exposure badges."

"When do we leave port?" Brian asks.

"The ship will leave Portsmouth Harbor on Monday morning, but you and Janey won't be on the crew during phase one, son. I need your quarters for the EPA lads. You two go get some beach time and join me on board during phase two."

"But you won't have a cook," Janey says.

"I've hired one, lass. When you join the crew during phase two, you'll be promoted to my marine biological technical adviser."

"You'll miss my Irish stew."

"Aye, but I'll be asking you to make that lovely concoction for our celebration after all those precious metals are safely on board."

"Tell us about phase two, the salvaging of the gold and platinum, Sean."

"I thought you might be interested in that, Pete. I've put together a sharing plan. Seventy percent of the gold and platinum proceeds go to my boat and crew, and thirty percent go to the crew of the *Elizabeth Ann lll.* Is that fair?"

They have the present day value of the quantity gold and platinum, shown on the manifest, in mind; Pete and Janey are quick to agree to Sean's proposal. Antonio follows their accord with a nod.

CHAPTER 25

On board the Sea Adventure in the Gulf of Maine

Kevin Fortuna sits in front of a console in the ROV control module. Justin McNulty, an apprentice ROV pilot looks over his shoulder. They are concentrating on the video coming to the monitor from the *Super Mohawk* ROV as it approaches the *Beddington*. The ROV lights play on bits of silt that resemble a snowstorm caught in a car's headlights. Kevin is briefing McNulty.

"The purpose of this dive is to carefully explore the area around the wreck for hazards to the ROV and the salvage operation, Justin. And after that, we'll attempt to locate the metalized uranium ingots."

Justin calls out, as Kevin moves the joystick to actuate the thrusters and maneuver the *Super Mohawk* toward the *Beddington*. "Wow, look at those fishing nets wrapped around the ship's structure, Kevin. They must've been snagged from trawlers passing by. We wouldn't want our ROV to be caught in one of those."

"We'll program their location into the Baseline Acoustic Telemetry System (BATS), and the ROV will stay away from them. Keep your eyes on the readings from that Geiger counter we mounted on the front of the ROV. Looks like the ship broke in two when it hit bottom. All kinds of debris are lying nearby. Some of the cargo must've spilled out of a hold when the ship broke apart. I'm going to move in closer to that pile of material where the ship split open."

"Kevin, the Geiger counter meter is pegged off scale."

"Okay, let me get closer to that pile of wood and stuff where we're getting the high radiation readings. I'm going to activate the high pressure water jets on the ROV to clear away some silt, so we can see what's lying around."

After the silt clears, a group of metal ingots appear on the monitor.

Kevin yells out, "Bingo!"

After a few high fives between Kevin and Justin, they get on with the other purpose of this ROV dive. Kevin directs the large crane operator to drop the steel recovery box near the ingots. It will be in position to retrieve them with the manipulator arms of the *Super Mohawk* during its next dive.

* * *

The next morning, the salvage operation commences. The large and small crane operators are dressed in protective clothing, as well as the three men from the EPA. They have helmets with clear Lexan face masks. All five men look like aliens from outer space. The rest of the crew is behind a yellow caution tape, one hundred feet from the cranes. All have been issued radiation exposure badges. Five steel barrels lined with lead stand by on deck, ready to receive the metalized uranium ingots that will be lifted by the small crane from the retrieval box. Captain Kelly is on the bridge, and he'll keep the ship and cranes stabilized during the salvage operation.

The leader of the EPA group insisted on inspecting all the salvage equipment. His inspection is taking too long, and Captain Kelly is losing patience. He calls his first mate on the ship's phone. "Clancy, tell that idiot in the monkey suit to get on with it. I'd like to get this salvage underway before Saint Paddy's Day."

An hour later, the inspection is completed, and the salvage operation commences.

Kevin Fortuna and Justin McNulty are working the ROV control module, performing their prelaunch checks, making sure the signals through the umbilical attached to the *Super Mohawk* are operating. When Kevin finishes his checks, he gives the deck crew the order to launch the ROV.

Captain Sean Kelly's booming voice comes over the speaker in the ROV control module. "Don't lose that ROV, Kevin, or I'll have your ass. It cost me $900,000 as a used item."

Justin McNulty takes the heat from the captain's terse warning. His face turns beet red, and perspiration dots appear on his forehead. Kevin is unperturbed. It's a threat he's heard before, and he knows he'll hear it again.

The *Super Mohawk* slowly descends four hundred feet down to the metalized uranium. Kevin has both hands on the joysticks, making slight movements to activate the positioning thrusters until the ROV is near the pile of ingots.

"Okay, Justin. Let's deploy the manipulator arms and pick up our first one."

They watch the monitor as an arm from the *Super Mohawk* is positioned to reach out toward an ingot. The claw at the end of the arm opens and grasps it. The ROV moves a slight distance, carrying the ingot in its grasp until it's set gently into the retrieval box. This process is repeated until the retrieval box is loaded with seven more, weighing fifty pounds each.

Kevin radios the large crane operator and says, "Andy, lift the first load."

When the retrieval box reaches the deck, the small crane operator lifts each ingot and places all eight, one by one, into a lead-lined steel barrel marked with a red radiation symbol. The EPA men, in their protective gear, put a cover on the barrel and seal it.

This salvage procedure is repeated four more times until all five barrels are filled, sealed, and weighed. The head EPA man verifies that one ton of radioactive metalized uranium has been salvaged and safely secured.

The retrieval box, cranes, the deck, protective clothing, and the *Super Mohawk* are power washed, and a Geiger counter test is made for any remaining radiation contamination. There is none. The crew turns in their radiation exposure badges, and they're developed by the EPA men. All are negative.

The *Sea Adventure* leaves the Gulf of Maine and heads for Portsmouth Harbor. When they arrive six hours later, the five steel barrels containing the metalized uranium are off-loaded to a waiting van. The van leaves Portsmouth for an undisclosed location.

After the ship is secure, Captain Sean Kelly and Kevin Fortuna walk down the gangplank. When they reach the wharf, Kelly says, "Well, Kevin, it was a good job getting that salvage safely over with. Will your joystick wrists be ready in three days for our phase two salvage job?"

"Captain Kelly, the retrieval of gold and platinum bars will be more soothing to my sore joystick wrists than those metalized uranium ingots were."

CHAPTER 26

The *Sea Adventure* is back in the Gulf of Maine, getting ready to initiate phase two of the salvage operation, recovering the gold and platinum from hold number four of the *SS Beddington*.

Kevin Fortuna sits at a console in the ROV module. He's reviewing a video of the wreck below. Brian Kelly and Justin McNulty watch the display as the *Beddington*'s features, from bow to stern, pass by. Janey Sheffield stands as an interested observer behind the seated ROV pilot and his two apprentices.

"Janey, do me a favor," Kevin says. "Go to the bridge and get that diagram of the ship's structure that was in the package. I want to plan a *Super Mohawk* mission and approach into hold number four where the manifest tells us the gold and platinum are stowed."

Janey returns with the diagram, and they gather around a table where it's spread.

Kevin points to a place on the diagram with his pen. "The ship broke in half between holds number three and four. That's why that ton of metalized uranium was tossed out of hold three...right here. Don't understand how it broke out of those wooden barrels scattered all around there."

"Doesn't look like gold or platinum flipped out of hold number four, Kevin."

"Right, Brian, so the *Super Mohawk* will have to enter hold four to find and retrieve it."

Kevin stands up. He staggers before he sits again.

"Kevin, are you okay?" Janey asks.

"I'm just a little dizzy."

"You didn't eat anything today. Do you have any pain?"

"Yeah, I'm hurting right here." He points to the right side of his abdomen. Kevin slumps down in his chair. "Damn! It's hurting worse. Shit! Why now? Just when I'm due to get that platinum and gold up."

Brian grabs the ships phone and calls the bridge. "Dad, Kevin's sick and in pain."

"I'll be right there. Make him lie down."

Captain Kelly rushes into the ROV module with a first aid kit in hand. He feels Kevin's brow. "He's hot." He puts a thermometer in Kevin's mouth. "Wow...one hundred and two. I'll give him a couple of aspirin for the pain and fever."

"Don't do that, Captain Kelly."

"Why not, lass?"

"I think he's having an appendicitis attack. According to my first aid training, he shouldn't eat or drink anything."

"What can we do for him, Florence Nightingale?"

"Captain Kelly, he's got to get to a hospital for surgery before the appendix bursts and peritonitis results", Janey says.

"Is that it?"

"We need to put him on a stretcher and place an ice bag on the area of pain. She answers.

"We're over eighty miles at sea, lass, and, at least, that far from a hospital. Okay, I've got to call the Coast Guard for a helicopter evacuation." Kelly leaves the ROV and rushes up to the bridge to make the call.

Captain Kelly returns with a stretcher. "The Coast Guard at Sandwich on Cape Cod has a Jayhawk chopper in the air, heading for the ship. It'll be here in ninety minutes. We need to get Kevin out on deck to wait."

Brian grabs one end of the stretcher with Justin McNulty on the other. They move Kevin outside to the deck. When they set him down, Janey is there with an ice bag and a blanket. Kevin beckons to Brian, and he kneels down beside him.

"Your dad will want to abort the gold and platinum salvage operation because I'm not there to pilot the ROV. You can do it, Brian. With the break between hold number three and four, it won't be difficult to pilot the ROV right into hold four. Look at the recorded videos of that opening and watch out for obstructions."

While in pain, Kevin spends the next half hour briefing Brian on the ROV dive to hold number four. He's interrupted by the sound of the helicopter coming toward the ship.

Captain Kelly approaches the stretcher with a survival suit. He whispers to Brian. "Let's get Kevin into this. The swells are running about seven feet. In case he's dumped in the cold water, he'll be okay in this."

Janey, Brian, Captain Kelly, and the crew watch as the chopper hovers seventy feet above the deck. They see a rescue basket being let down toward the ship suspended by a cable. It's swinging, and the coast guard rescue swimmer in the door of the chopper is having a hard time aiming it to the deck of the *Sea Adventure* because of the up and down motion of the ship and the wind effect.

The *Jayhawk* crew makes several attempts to land the basket on deck, but the swells and wind still counter their effort.

Janey asks Captain Kelly. "What if they can't get the basket down on deck?"

"I'll assign you to perform the surgery to remove the appendix."

She puts a hand to her mouth with a shocked expression on her face and stammers. "You will?"

Janey gives a long sigh of relief when the basket with the rescue swimmer finally reaches the deck after two more attempts. Two crew members from the ship strap Kevin in. He's hoisted up to the open chopper door. The cable and basket are more stable with Kevin and the swimmers weight on the way up than it was on the way down. A *Jayhawk* crewman hauls in the basket. The chopper door closes, and the *Jayhawk* speeds away toward Cape Cod Hospital in Hyannis, Massachusetts.

Brian is still on deck when he notices the crew preparing to get underway. He rushes up to the bridge and confronts his father. "Dad, you're not leaving the salvage site, are you?"

"I've got to return to port and delay it. We don't have an ROV pilot. I called the company that makes the *Super Mohawk*, and it'll be three weeks before one of their pilots can get here."

"If you delay the salvage that long, we'll have to contend with October weather. I can pilot the ROV, find the gold and platinum, and bring it up."

"You've got to be kidding, Brian. You've never piloted an ROV in a salvage operation. I can't afford to lose a $900,000 ROV."

"I've run simulations and been involved with Kevin on ROV dives. I've even operated the joystick to control a dive. Kevin briefed me on this salvage operation, and Justin McNulty has a good feel for it. We can do it, Dad."

"Okay, I was going to leave this evening, but I'll hold off until morning. I want you and McNulty to meet me in the ROV control module in an hour. I'll evaluate your dive plan and make my decision to continue the salvage operation based on that."

Brian leaves the bridge and looks for Justin McNulty. He finds him in the ship's galley, having coffee with Janey.

"Hey, Justin. Let's get to the ROV module. I have to prove that we can pilot the ROV and salvage the gold and platinum. My old man will be there in an hour."

"Brian, may I make a suggestion?"

"Sure, Janey. Suggest away."

"First, from what I know about your dad, he'll want to question you and Justin about every detail concerning the dive and recovery. He knows a lot about running a ship, but little about piloting an ROV. I'll play the part of Captain Kelly. Let's get over to the ROV module."

* * *

"Okay, show me on the *Beddington's* structural diagram where the ROV will enter hold number four," Janey says, playing the part of Captain Kelly.

Brian points to the area between hold three and four. He smiles while saying, "Right here, Dad."

"That's the way the ship's structure looked before it was sunk, son. How about the way it looks now?"

Brian wheels his chair over to a display showing a still photo taken by the *Super Mohawk* of the split between hold four and three on the *Beddington*. "This is where the ROV will enter hold four."

"Is there room to maneuver the ROV through that split and into four?"

"Yes, Dad. We did a simulation of that. I'll show you." Brian's fingers hit on the keypad until the simulated run of the ROV through the gap between three and four comes up on the display.

"Okay, Brian. Show me the ROV dive route you'll take from the surface down four hundred feet to hold number four."

"I can bring that up on the display. This is not a simulation; it's a video of an actual ROV dive to that area." Brian types for a few seconds until the *Super Mohawk's* cameras show the slow decent of the ROV down toward hold number four. "I was the ROV pilot during this dive."

"Wait, Brian. What about all those fishing nets? Are you sure the ROV won't get snagged by one?"

"Yes, Justin plotted their location, and they're programmed into the dive profile by BATS, so the *Super Mohawk* won't get close."

"Kevin warned us about the current down there that's running at four knots an hour. He said it can whip around the *Super Mohawk's* umbilical cord and get it tangled in the ship's structure. If that should occur, Mister ROV Pilot, how would you untangle it and save my ROV?"

"Hard to explain, Dad. I guess I'd move the ROV in and around the tangle until it was undone."

Janey's devil's advocacy continues. "How about salvaging the ingots? Where will the crane operator place the retrieval box, so it can take on the gold and platinum?"

Again, Brian's fingers fly over the keyboard. The simulated position of the retrieval box is shown hanging on a cable, as Brian says, "The cable will clear the ship's structure."

Janey twists an imaginary handlebar mustache, and, in a deep, stern voice, says, "Okay, that's enough, son. You lads don't know what the fuck you're doing, and you'll probably leave my $900,000 ROV on the bottom of the freakin' briny."

After that remark by Janey, all three in the ROV module laugh to vent the tension accumulated during the last hour.

* * *

Later, Janey waits on deck outside the ROV module for Captain Kelly to come out. After being in there with Brian and Justin for half an hour, he leaves and rushes by her, toward the bridge, intent on getting a report on Kevin's condition from Cape Cod Hospital. Brian and Justin follow him out the door.

"How did it go, Brian?" Janey asks.

"Piece of cake. My dad's questions were easier than yours. We start salvaging the gold and platinum in the morning."

They go up to the bridge. They're eager to know about Kevin. When they enter, Kelly is closing his cell phone. "The operation was a success, and Kevin's okay. He'll not be back on board for two weeks." Kelly puts a hand on his son's shoulder. "Okay, Mister ROV Pilot... you've got the joysticks."

CHAPTER 27

The next morning, the ROV is launched. Brian sits at the console with his hands on the joysticks, making slight movements to activate the thrusters controlling the descent of the *Super Mohawk*. Justin adjusts the display to present a clear picture of its dive down to hold number four. Janey stands behind the console, watching the display as the dive proceeds.

Captain Kelly's voice blares out from the ROV module's intercom. "Brian, I just got an updated weather message. According to the American and European hurricane tracking models, Hurricane David will be on top of us in thirty-four hours. You've got to find those precious metals and get them on deck in twenty-six hours. I want to get this ship out of here and headed back to Portsmouth before that storm hits us."

Brian swallows hard and grabs the microphone. "I should be able to do that."

After Captain Kelly's hurricane warning commanding a strict salvage time window, the mood in the control module is tense. Brian seems to be gripping the joysticks tighter. Justin rolls his eyes, and sweat appears on his brow.

Janey grips Brian's right shoulder and massages the back of his neck while he controls the ROV's slow dive toward hold four. She attempts to cool the tension by commenting on the spectacular view shown by the ROV cameras on the display. "Wow, I feel like I'm inside the ROV. Look, the lights are picking up all those fish. The ship really is an artificial reef, providing an ecosystem for all that marine life. Hey, guys! There's the place where the ship split between hold three and four. Wonder why all those pieces of wood are scattered about. It looks almost like someone or something smashed up a bunch of barrels."

Janey and Justin are quiet while watching the *Super Mohawk* ease its way toward the opening into hold four. They don't want to interfere with Brian's concentration during this critical point in the dive.

"Shit! The umbilical cord is being pushed around by the current," Brian shouts. "Look, the cord moved in front of the ROV. Damn! Its formed a loop." He moves the joystick, so the thrusters will make the *Super Mohawk* back away, and the loop will straighten out. Too late...the umbilical cord loop, still caught in the current, passes over the ROV and snags on a section of the broken ship's hull.

After an hour attempting to untangle the umbilical cord, the voice Brian didn't want to hear booms in over the ROV module speaker. "What's going on, Brian? I haven't heard any word about the dive."

"The umbilical cord is tangled. I'm working on straightening it out."

"Great! I've got a hurricane coming at my ship, I'm about to lose a $900,000 ROV and abort a salvage operation. I'll be right there."

"Please don't come! Let me work to get the cord untangled without you hanging over my shoulder."

There's a pause on the intercom before Kelly senior says, "Okay, I'll be in the galley waiting for some good news."

"Janey, do me a favor. Go to the galley and keep my father calm and away from here."

"Okay, Brian. You can untangle it. Call me on the intercom when you get it done."

* * *

Janey sits at the large stainless steel table in the galley with Captain Kelly. Two hours pass with no word from the ROV module. Kelly's first mate enters the galley with an update on the hurricane.

"Sir, Hurricane David has picked up speed. It is now a category three still headed in our direction. We are getting some of the rainbands, and the sea is starting to get rough."

"When will the full force of that freakin' storm get here, Clancy?"

"According to the coast guard weather report, the outer fringe will be here in fourteen hours. We need seven hours to make port in Portsmouth. So, we've got to leave here no later than seven hours from now."

"Okay, Clancy. Have the crew batten down all the ship's equipment not being used in the salvage operation. Stay on the hurricane reports and alert me to any changes."

Kelly starts to pace back and forth. He stops to look at a barometer on the wall. "This freakin' glass is falling. The storm is coming straight at us."

He waits ten more minutes before he says, "That's enough time. He's not going to get the cord untangled. I'll have to cut it, dump the ROV, and get the hell out of here."

"Captain, shame on you. You should have more faith in your son. Kevin Fortuna told us that it takes time to untangle an ROV umbilical cord."

"We don't have time, lass. I've got to get this ship to safe harbor before that hurricane gets here. The way I look at it, Brian has an hour to get that umbilical untangled. It will take, at least, six hours to complete the salvage operation, if there is one. Then, it will take seven hours to pull anchor and make it to port."

* * *

In the ROV module, Brian is attempting a different maneuver with the *Super Mohawk* to try and untangle the umbilical cord when his father's voice booms over the intercom speaker. "Brian, you've got fifty-five minutes to get that cord untangled!"

Brian stands up from the console and pulls the speaker from the wall. He throws it and the microphone across the room. Then, he sits back down.

"Justin, I've got the umbilical unsnagged from the ship. Now, I'm going to try something to get the cord behind the ROV. I'm going to move it through that loop it made earlier."

"That's going to make a knot in the cord, Brian."

"I know, but Kevin told me that, sometimes, it's the only way to get the cord behind the ROV. He said the umbilical can survive a knot."

Brian moves the joystick, so the thrusters send the *Super Mohawk* through the loop. Then, he moves it up. Justin holds his breath and releases it when the knot forms and the umbilical cord trails behind the ROV.

"Okay. Now, I'll carefully maneuver into hold four."

A few minutes later, he says, "I'm in there. Justin, call my dad on the intercom and tell him to come here."

"You broke the intercom, Brian."

Brian smiles. "Oh, yeah! Go to the galley, dude, and tell him to come."

It took Captain Kelly and Janey only seven seconds to rush from the galley to the ROV module.

BILL FLYNN

"I've untangled the cord, Dad, and the ROV is in hold four. I'm
going to move it around there to look for the gold and platinum."

"I knew you could do it, lad."

"Oh, yeah? How come I didn't get that from you earlier?"

After a few minutes of searching hold four, Captain Kelly says,
"Hey, hold number four is looking empty to me. All I see is a
bunch of smashed up barrels."

"Wait! Brian, move the *Super Mohawk* to the right. I saw a stack
of something right there." Janey points to it on the display.

Brian tweaks the joysticks, activating the thrusters, so the ROV
faces the object Janey called out. The bright lights of the ROV
shine on a pile of brick-like items. One side of the pile is golden
in color and the other a dull gray. "It looks like they could be gold
and platinum ingots. Justin, activate the Geiger counter."

Justin touches a switch on the console. "I'm only getting a little
background radiation, Brian. It's nothing like the readings we got
from those metalized uranium canisters."

"Good, but that small stack is nowhere near the four tons of
gold and platinum that's supposed to be in hold four. Hang on,
there's a sign near that pile of ingots. I'll try to get in close enough
to read it."

He moves the *Super Mohawk*, so it approaches within two feet of
the sign. The ROV hovers there and activates its high pressure jets
to clear the silt. When the camera is focused and the ROV's lights
aimed, some words and an image appear.

Captain Kelly, Janey, Brian, and Justin glare at the display.
They're stunned for a few seconds before Janey says, "What in the
hell do those odd words with that eerie drawing mean?"

Captain Kelly's expression turns to a grimace as he answers her. "It means someone got here before us."

They all glare at the image on the display. The camera plays on the stack of gold and platinum ingots, and it pans to a nearby bulkhead where there're strange words with a crude drawing of a weird, little character.

CHAPTER 28

Captain Kelly's voice roars through the repaired speaker in the ROV module. "We've unloaded the last of the gold and platinum bars from the retrieval box, Brian. Good job! We've got to recover the ROV and weigh anchor. There's just enough time to make port before the hurricane hits here."

* * *

It's a rough trip back to Portsmouth with ten foot seas and high winds buffeting the *Sea Adventure*. Janey is at the bow as the ship pummels through the waves. The bow is always her favorite place on the *Elizabeth Ann lll* in rough seas. She's wearing a yellow rain slicker and the hood of the rain slicker covers her hair as the sea spray hits. Brian joins her.

"Hey! What are you doing here?" he yells above the roar of the ocean. "Do you like the bow in rough weather as much I do?" He puts his arm around her and removes her hood. Brian touches her face and traces a rivulet of mist from her cheek to her lips before they kiss. The mist blowing in from white capped waves doesn't bother them, and, this time, there's no interruption by the ship's fog horn. Brian takes her hand, and they walk the wallowing deck toward the shelter of their quarters and a warm shower.

* * *

The *Sea Adventure* arrives in Portsmouth harbor at ten in the evening after seven hours of plowing through large waves. The tired crew retires to their quarters while the hurricane passes well to their east. Captain Kelly puts the weighing of the gold and platinum, along with any celebration, on hold until the morning.

* * *

Brian and Janey arrive on deck to sunshine and blue skies with the crew of the *Sea Adventure*. They're all waiting for Captain Kelly to announce the total value of the gold and platinum.

Once the last of the gold and platinum ingots are weighed, Captain Kelly busily calculates the total worth of that one ton of precious metals.

"Okay, here's what we have at today's prices." He has the results of his calculated totals written in a notebook. He reads: "The grand total is $41,160,000."

A loud cheer fills the *Sea Adventure*. A crew member puts Brian on Justin's shoulders, and it's high fives all around.

Kelly's fingers touch his calculator once more. "This is the share for the crew of the *Elizabeth Ann lll* at thirty percent." He shows the number to Janey. It's $12,364,800.

Janey gasps and takes the cell phone from her jean jacket pocket and she calls Peter Broderick. After he answers, she says, "Guess what?"

"Quite a storm. Antonio and I rode it out on the *Elizabeth Ann*. Were you guys in port before it hit?"

"Yeah, we just made it in."

"How did the salvage go? Did you get it done before the storm? You caught me in the car going to Logan Airport to pick up Jimmy Lawson. He's coming in from England. What have you got, Janey?"

"You, Antonio, and I are millionaires!"

"You guys brought up the gold and platinum? Awesome!"

"Yeah, some of it was missing, but we got enough."

"What's the *Elizabeth Ann lll's* share?"

"We're in for over twelve million."

"You're kidding!"

"No, I'm not. You can buy a new trawler and Antonio can travel Portugal."

"Will anyone else claim part of it...like the Russians or the Brits?"

"According to Captain Kelly's lawyer they can try, but they won't be successful. Remember that cover up in 1945? The *SS Beddington* is a phantom ship. All records of its existence were destroyed. Hey! We're in Portsmouth, and the party has started, Pete. I'll see you in a couple of days. I could be carrying a check for over twelve million dollars if Captain Kelly can get it all sorted out by then. By the way, Brian is great...I think I'll marry him."

"Speaking of marriage...Jimmy Lawson, the survivor from the *Beddington*, wants to marry my aunt Annie. They're both eighty-six. How about that?"

"Good for them. Hey! Some strange things happened during the salvage. Someone else got most of the gold and platinum— more than three tons out of the four on that manifest. They left a weird sign behind in hold number four. Captain Kelly says it was a slogan used all over Europe during World War Two."

"What did the sign say?"

"It said *KILROY WAS HERE.* There's also a cartoonlike character of a little man with a big nose hanging his hands over a wall. I think it was some kind of bizarre message left behind by whomever salvaged most of gold and platinum before we got here."

"I've seen those words and that little guy before. Who would've salvaged most of it and left a strange sign like that behind? Why didn't they take all that gold and platinum?"

"I don't have a clue, Captain Pete."

CHAPTER 29

Munich, Germany...October, 25^{th,} *2013*
Law offices of Wattenberg, Wattenberg & Associates.

The law office patriarch, Klaus Wattenberg, age eighty-seven, is acquainting his great-grandson, Hans, age twenty-five and a recent law school graduate, with the firm's current clients. The sage, old attorney has a head of flowing white hair that extends down to the collar of his tweed suit. He's puffing on a white meerschaum pipe.

Hans is six feet tall with short, blond hair. His good-looking facial features have been bronzed during an after-graduation holiday in Spain. Today, his first day at the firm, he wears a vested dark suit and a serious expression on that suntanned face.

"Sir, there are three cabinets of files marked Haupt/Meyer. How come?"

"The families of Haupt and Meyer are important clients."

"What businesses are they involved in?"

"Well, for the most part, it's construction. But their story is a long one. Let's have lunch while I tell you about them."

* * *

Hans and his great-grandfather sit a table in the Ratskeller on Marien Platz, near their office. The elder Wattenberg has been coming for lunch to this historical Munich restaurant, which first opened in 1874, since he started the law firm. He still savors the Ratskeller atmosphere on every visit. Today, as always, his bright blue eyes roam the restaurant, examining the dark mahogany tables, wide plank oak floors, shiny copper bar, and the bustling waiters, wearing white aprons adorned with black vertical stripes. He pauses to take it all in again before he calls a waiter over to order a half-liter stein of Spatenbrau beer and a yeager schnitzel for both of them.

When the beer arrives at their table, Klaus Wittenberg takes a large swallow of the golden brew. "I'll start at the beginning with Haupt and Meyer. I was your age when I started practicing law. Germany was rebuilding at that time after being defeated and brought to its knees by the Allied onslaught."

"I know all that dark history. Tell me about the Haupt and Meyer families."

Klaus takes a sip of his beer and smiles. "You're well-honed on badgering your witness to get them straight at the point. You'd make a good defense lawyer, Hans. Okay, Heinz Haupt and Gerhardt Meyer first came to me in 1952. They were forming a salvage company and wanted me to draw up their partnership. Later, I helped them lease a two hundred foot fishing trawler, which they outfitted with cranes and other deep sea salvage equipment, including a sonar system used in the war."

"What did they do during the war?"

"Ah, that's the key question, Hans. Haupt commanded a U-boat, and Meyer was his first mate. They'd torpedoed a ship, the SS Beddington, in 1945 off the coast of Maine. They knew the ship went down with four tons of precious metals consisting of gold and platinum. Haupt recorded the coordinates of that ship after he torpedoed it."

"So, he planned to salvage the ship? How deep?"

"Four hundred feet."

"That's deep. I've done some recreational diving in Spain, and we'd never go down more than thirty feet. We were warned about compression sickness and nitrogen narcosis. Since remote operated vehicles were not invented back then, how did they dive to the wreck?"

"They acquired a diving bell that was used to rescue crews in sunken U-boats. They modified it for a deep salvage operation."

"How were Haupt and Meyer going to work at four hundred feet?"

The schnitzel was served with two more steins of beer. Klaus took two bites, chewed the tender veal, and washed it down with Spatenbrau before he answered. "I'm not proficient in diving bell technology, but here's what they told me. They modified the diving bell with an air lock transfer chamber, a decompression chamber that would hold four divers, a storage bin for food, tools, and spare breathing gas cylinders."

"Wait a minute. What did they breathe? Oxygen at that depth wouldn't work?"

"The canisters they used outside the diving bell in helmeted dive suits were filled with eighty-percent helium and twenty percent oxygen. They practiced for a year in the North Sea with a diving crew going in and out of the bell at four-hundred feet. Two divers would work outside the bell while the other two were decompressing and resting after their shift."

"Did both Haupt and Meyer work out of the diving bell?"

"No, Haupt managed the crew onboard the ship while Meyer was down below in the diving bell, handling the salvage operation. The ship's company and divers were mostly made up from Haupt's wartime crew on U-873."

"So, how did their salvage operation go?"

Klaus finishes the last bite of schnitzel and takes a swallow of beer. He answers, "Well, the trawler departed Bremerhaven and reached the coordinates Haupt recorded in the Gulf of Maine. They started searching the bottom with sonar for the wreck."

"Wouldn't that salvage effort be sensitive to the Americans even though it was seven years after the war?"

"Not really. They were operating in international waters, and their ship resembled a fishing trawler. There were no incidents."

"Okay, did they salvage that gold and platinum from the *Beddington?*"

"It took them two weeks before they located the ship with their sonar because it was several miles from the position Haupt had recorded in 1945."

"And after they located it, what happened?"

"They marked the wreck's location with a buoy and went in to Portland, Maine, for provisions. That's when Haupt called, asking me to file a claim on his behalf for the right to salvage the cargo."

"Did you get it claimed?"

"When I started to process the claim, the normal course of doing so took an unexpected turn. There wasn't any record of the *Beddington* anywhere. It was a British ship, according to Haupt. The precious metal cargo came from Russia and was being shipped to the United States as a Lend-Lease payback. I even queried *Lloyd's of London,* who've records on all merchant ships. They didn't show anything on the *Beddington.* There was no way for me to process a claim for a ship that didn't exist."

"It sounds like there was a cover up by the Americans for some reason. What else was on the *Beddington* besides the gold and platinum?"

"According to Haupt, uranium ore was onboard. It was taken from Strassfurt in 1945 by the Americans."

"That could've been the reason for a cover-up. Anyway, did Haupt proceed with the salvage?"

"They brought up three tons of platinum and gold, Hans."

"I thought there were four tons there. What happened to the rest?"

"An equipment problem developed to make them abort the salvage operation before they got it all. The crane that was used to bring up the box loaded with ingots broke down and couldn't be repaired."

"With a ton of gold and platinum ready for the taking there, I'd be interested."

"You're too late, Hans. An attorney acquaintance of mine from Portsmouth, New Hampshire informed me that its been salvaged."

"So Haupt and Meyer salvaged three tons of platinum and gold and left the area."

"Not quite. When Haupt and Meyer returned to our defeated country after the war, they saw some weird signs left by the Americans on buildings all over Germany. As a last gesture, before they left the *Beddington* site, the divers placed that same sign in the ship's hold from where they'd taken most of the platinum and gold."

"What did the sign say?"

"It said, '*Kilroy Was Here*.'"

"I've seen that on some old buildings in Munich. They probably thought someone would salvage the rest of the platinum and gold eventually and left that message for them to ponder. Maybe Meyer and Haupt wanted to claim victory, just like the invading American army did with their Kilroy signs. Did you continue to represent Haupt and Meyer?"

Klaus called the waiter and ordered apple strudel and coffee for them before he answered, "Yes, when they returned, I was asked for advice relative to selling the platinum and gold."

"What advice did you give them?"

"It was most likely some of the best advice I'd given anyone since I started the firm. I told them not to sell all of it. Instead, put the majority of the gold and platinum in a Swiss bank vault and use it as loan collateral for the construction business they planned on starting. The gold alone was selling for only thirty-seven dollars an ounce in 1952. Today, it's $1288 an ounce."

"Did Haupt and Meyer go into construction?"

"Yes, and Haupt was very successful at rebuilding our bombed out country."

"How about Meyer?"

"Sadly, he died from cancer six months after they returned from the salvage operation. It was assumed that he received high doses of radiation from some of the uranium on board the *Beddington*. Two other divers died of cancer soon after."

"What happened to Haupt?"

"Since he didn't take part in diving for the salvage, he wasn't exposed to the high levels of radiation. Heinz Haupt died ten years ago at eighty-seven. He provided well for his family and all those in the Meyer family. Everyone in the ship's crew and the divers' relatives were, also, taken care of."

"Is there any platinum and gold left in that Swiss bank vault?"

"Yes, most of the original deposit is still there. The descendants of Haupt and Meyer are still in the construction business and using that gold and platinum as collateral for construction loans. Right now, the total value of those precious metals stored in that Swiss bank vault is around $120,000,000."

"That's enough to sustain any business. So, I now know why we have three cabinets full of Haupt/Meyer files at the firm."

Klaus takes the last bite of his apple strudel, sips from his coffee, and lights his pipe. His blue eyes seem to laugh. "Yes, Hans. All those files belong to you. The Haupt and Meyer families will be your first clients."

THE END

Bill Flynn lives in New Hampshire with his wife, Barbara. When he's not writing, he plays imperfect golf on perfect golf courses, and fishes the Atlantic surf. He also travels the country with Barbara visiting five daughters and their families. Bill Flynn's email is: wflynn6782@comcast.net.

Made in the USA
Middletown, DE
28 October 2021